SIDEBITCH

LOWKEE

ACKNOWLEDGMENTS

To the real you, I'm glad you found yourself.
You couldn't have the first copy, so I gave you this page
instead.
You win.
Love you, forever.

SIDEBITCH

written by LowKee
based on a true story

ONE

Kiana, Obvi

ALEXA, play *The Weekend* by SZA. The Sidebitch Anthem. My, anthem. I don't say that with pride. I just speak facts. I'm a sidebitch. For context, we are defining 'sidebitch' as a woman who is not the main woman in a man's life. She doesn't get any real time. She's his best kept secret. The woman he runs to when he has time, needs pussy, or needs peace outside of his actual relationship, regardless, she's giving him some pussy. Society might even consider her a home-wrecker and/or a hoe. But I'm neither a home-wrecker nor a hoe. Granted, I have been dealing with a man who is practically married. I'm talking about living together, raising their children together, and running businesses together. The works. On top of that, they're what *Insta-*

gram likes to call 'Public Figures'. Probably a couple of your favorites. But to me, he's a regular nigga that I fell for before you had a chance to love him. Unfortunately for her, to me, she's always going to be the woman he said was a queen but she's crazy and he doesn't want to deal with her. I hold on to words. I remember conversations. That's probably how I got myself into this sidebitch role.

L et me introduce myself. I'm Kiana Sims. Thirty years old, an emotional Cancer, and a marketing executive at one of the biggest firms in L.A. I have my shit together. In L.A. terms, that means I pay my bills and buy my purses without sponsorship. Shorty is still working on that credit score, but you are too. I'm no 'Public Figure', but I'm connected. I have the best friends a girl could ask for. My 'love' life is rocky, obvi . But only because I'm stubborn and picky. Ok, I'm disregarding the fact that I'm dealing with a practically married man when I say I'm picky. Picky doesn't mean you always pick the right one. Anyway, I'm very single. I'm kinda mingling. But also kinda staying loyal to Mark, which is Brittany's boyfriend, not mine. I know, girl. What?.

I guess it's only right that I tell you a little bit about Mark before I tell you our story. But don't forget that I told you that he and Brittany are probably some of your favorites. Although I'm a sidebitch, I'm not a homewrecker, like I said. So, I'll keep some of the details to myself and let you fill in the blanks how you please. I'm not all the way messy. I also like to think of myself as privately petty. So this is just between us, right?

Mark Miller is in his thirties. Virgo. He happens to be one of the hardest working men that I've ever met. For the most part, he moves in silence. Keeps a tight lid on what he's doing until its necessary to be loud about it. He's talented. A great father. Well mannered. Strong in his spiritual beliefs. Free thinker. Also an overthinker. Smooth talker. Gentleman. Ladies' man. Chocolate skin. Stands at about six-two. Big dick. Sorry. Stay focused, sis. I met him through a mutual friend. At that time, I had no clue that at some point in his life, he was kind of a big deal in the NBA. When we met, he had just come out of a short marriage, he was a free agent, both figuratively and literally, and he was kind of just getting his life back to where he needed it to be.

I didn't care that he had been in the NBA. I didn't care about the amount of money he had touched in his life or how many houses he had at one point or another. I'm not that girl. He was tall, cute, my friend vouched for him, and we had a few other really solid mutual friends. So why the hell not? The night we met, we took a picture together and sent it to one of our mutual friends via *Snapchat*.

Both of us were pretty amazed to realize we had so many friends in common and had never crossed paths prior to that moment. At the risk of sounding corny, I'm going to say that moment, the entire moment, was pretty electric. With Bryson Tiller playing in the background, we had a number of random conversations about life, like kids, traveling, music, we cracked jokes, and we even discussed my prior experience in massage therapy. I don't usually tell men I used to be a massage therapist right away, because they typically accidentally let their minds wander really far, really fast. But it felt like Mark and I were already friends. In the short time that we had spent during the initial connection, we vibed. Hard. We exchanged some really dope energy and I liked it. So at the end of the night when he asked for my number because he 'needed to see what my massages were hitting for', I gave it to him.

That same night, we exchanged some playful banter through text messages because when I gave him my number, he also gave me his, and sent me a text that said, 'Mark'. So me being the smart ass that I am, replied with a text that said, "Kiana, obvi." We went back and forth with GIFs for a few messages and then we didn't communicate for a full month. I wasn't searching for Mr. Right, not even for Mr. Right Now, so I wasn't pressed. But I'll keep it all the way funky, I did think about him a few times over the course of that month.

One night, I had a super random dream and he and another mutual friend of ours was in it. The thing about me is that no dream of mine is ever actually random. My dreams always hold meaning, so if I dream about it, I absolutely pay attention to it. I ended up hitting him up to tell him how random it was. I sent him my *Bitmoji* peeking through some blinds as my opening text, just to check his temperature. I won't lie, I was a tad nervous when I sent it because this felt like I was putting in too much work. I'm not typically the aggressor in situations. I've never had to be. I sent the message and waited eight hours for a reply. I felt so stupid.

To my surprise, when he finally replied, he replied with a *Bitmoji* too. Weird shit like that is fun for me. I like when men entertain my foolery without needing to be prompted to do so. I mean, I definitely could have done without the eight hour delay but, to me, that means we have the same warped sense of humor, which always makes things more fun. Anyway, once we got the *Bitmoji* thing out of the way, I told him he was in my dream and his response was, "LOL, dang I'm already in your dreams, get used to it!" I told him not to get carried away, he was just walking around Walmart. Which was true, but I wasn't ready for him to be so gassed by it, so I had to humble him right quick.

That sparked some flirtatious conversation and then he told me I had a smart mouth that he needed to fix. Right after he sent that text, he sent another that said, "This is probably inappropriate, but fuck it," and sent a meme that was a picture of a woman being fucked from behind while the man told her how much shit she talked. Whew! I wasn't ready, but I quickly replied, "Yeah, we'll see. I mean, ain't nobody fixed it yet".

. . .

Our story started the night we met, but the show started the moment I replied to that text. I would actually call it a sick season of *Love & Hip Hop*. But I'm not a rapper and he was never in love. So there's that. The beginning of our story is basic, so I'll get through it quickly so that I can really get you into the good stuff.

Okay, so, where was I? Oh, we ended up planning a visit. I'm telling you the vibe between us and the energy we exchanged was different. I don't know if it's because of the mutual friends we shared and the unspoken idea of how close we were to each of those people had meant we should have met sooner, or if it was because of how quickly we clicked when we first met, but it was like we had been friends for years. Like, the level of comfort I felt with him that early on was wild. Even wilder, is that I could feel that the feeling was mutual.

So, inviting him over to my house as our first official 'hang out' didn't even make me feel any type of way. We all know that's a no-no under any other circumstance. Let me be very clear, it's not easy to catch my attention and it's even harder to keep it. I am also the most challenging person when it comes to letting people in. But once you're in, I'm an open book. I'm also weird about allowing men to know where I live, so the fact that I was one thousand percent comfortable with inviting him over spoke volumes to me.

. . .

W hen he got to my place, I went out to get him. He embraced my body with a hug that felt natural. As we walked upstairs to my apartment, he was on *FaceTime* with his daughter, so he lingered in the hallway for a while after I went in to my apartment. When he finally walked in, he physically kept his distance, as if all five feet, five inches of me posed some sort of threat. I jokingly pressed him about it, but I expected a real answer. "Why do you run away whenever I get near you?"

His response was, in true playa fashion, "'Cus I forgot how you looked, now I gotta keep my distance to control myself." We both laughed.

"That sounds like a personal problem, sir. But you don't need to control anything. This is me guaranteeing your safety. Nothing is going to happen. I'm not that girl. Even if I was, it's a bye week, so we're good". As we were having that conversation, I was setting up my massage table. After all, when we set this meeting up, it was for massage purposes only. I mean, we're all adults and I wouldn't have done anything sexual with him this early anyway, but with the sexual energy added to the dope vibe and already otherwise electric energy we shared, I felt the need to let him know that it was that time of the month, so that he knew he was staying on the bench this quarter.

He sat on the couch playing in his phone while I draped the massage table with linens and when I was done, I said, "Okay, strip," which obviously caught him off guard because all he could say was, "Oh, shit."

We both laughed and I said, "I'm just kidding – well kinda – because you do have to take your clothes off, you just don't have to do it like a stripper."

To my surprise, Mark said, "I'm not getting a massage anymore, I changed my mind." He didn't even look up from his phone when he said it. He didn't crack even the smallest bit of a smile.

I laughed hysterically. Ole scaredy-cat ass. He continued, "I really was going to get one, but I haven't seen you in so long that I for real forgot how fine you are and now I can't do it." By that time, he was looking me in the eyes while he spoke to me.

So I said, "I already set up the table, you're getting a massage. So, do you need help taking your clothes off or what?" Then I walked over to him on the couch and he got up and walked in the other direction. We were literally walking around the massage table laughing like children because this man was being so childish. Eventually, I stood on top of the table and got on his back. At that point, we were both being childish. Finally, I was able to convince him to strip down to his *Ethikas*.

He got on the table, played a spa station on his phone, took a deep breath, and seemingly prepared his mind for relaxation. I wasn't nervous or anything because massage was and still is one of my favorite things to do. I was just surprised that we were even in that space and shaking my head because we really acted like children to get him on top of that table. It was silly fun, but I think it aided in the level of comfort we had toward one another. I gave him a full body hour-long massage, minus his feet because he kept his socks on. For the most part, he slept, which in massage world is one of the greatest compliments. At one point, he woke up and said, "Yo, you could really make some money off this, get you a little speaker, a candle and a little table so that you can have a nice little set up."

I just giggled and kept massaging. I didn't want to make a conversation of it while he was supposed to be in a state of relaxation, but him saying that, let me know I was doing a good job. When I was done, he slowly got up and I said, "I'll close my eyes while you get dressed."

We both laughed as he put his clothes back on. Once he was fully dressed, he said, "See, you gone be a problem!"

I casually replied, "I don't create problems, I solve them." I walked to the kitchen after that to wash my hands and let him sit with his thoughts. When I returned to the living room, he was on the phone with his best friend, bragging about how fine I was and how great the massage was that I had just given him.

After that, we sat on the couch and talked. One more thing you should know about Mark is that he isn't neces- sarily a liar, but he does withhold copious amounts of usually pertinent information. Anyway, while we were talking, I asked an extremely important question. "Do you have a girlfriend or does any woman in the streets think that she is your girlfriend?"

W ith a dead serious face, he replied, "Yeah, I didn't tell you that?" Ok, at that point, he was sitting on my couch, so I was a little late. But, if he was going to lie about it, he would have done it the night we met or the day he sat on my couch. So, stall me out.

Bitch, I was shook. With a smile on my face, I rolled my eyes and replied, "No, of course you didn't. You wouldn't be sitting on my couch if you did."

B ut he was only joking. So, his real answer was, "Nah, I actually just got out of a situation with a young lady. She's dope. She's a queen and a great mom. But she got some baby daddy issues that I don't necessarily wanna deal with and some other shit. She's also an actress. That's cool, but I don't really want to be with somebody in the industry and she's crazy too. I'm not big on that."

That's how he put Miss Brittany Vasquez on my radar. I'm the queen of research. Men like to call it stalking and I just feel like that has too much of a negative connotation, especially when all of the information was basically put on my desk for me to rummage through. So, based on his description of her, the other shit that I removed from this story, and with a little time spent looking through his comments and at his followers, I was able to figure out who his last mystery woman was. That sounds excessive, but I like to know what I'm dealing with and half of you are probably just as good, if not better researchers than I am.

Please note that this woman is not his ex-wife. He was married to the mother of his child and actually left that part out until a few days later. Perhaps he didn't want to spring everything on me at once. Perhaps he's just a typical nigga who leaves shit like this out even though it's a very crucial part of his history. Who knows.

Anyway, the next day he called me, and when my phone rang, I found myself smiling at the sight of his name on my screen. That's totally not my thing. I'm never pressed and hard to impress. "Well, hello, Mark Miller. Fancy seeing your name in my phone," I answered.

Without missing a beat, he said, "Man, I don't know what you did to me, but I haven't stopped thinking about you since yesterday. I'm just thinking like, if I make her mine, do I get that kinda treatment whenever I want?"

I was super fucking flattered. I mean, just a *Kool-Aid* smile from ear to ear, but I had to keep my cool, so I was just like, "Oh, it's definitely a boyfriend perk."

He said, "I figured it was. Ya resume looking real strong right now. I'm gonna keep watching though."

. . .

I liked that. I liked that he was still interested even after I turned his passive-aggressive sex talk down. I liked that he was referencing the future. I liked that he was even bringing up the idea of me being his. Call me naive. I don't care. Men talk 'in the future' to me all of the time, but when it came out of his mouth, it felt genuine. He was a smooth talker, but I could feel when he was being genuine and that's what stuck with me.

Alright, so fast forward a few weeks into this whole adventure. I say adventure because at that point, it was not a situationship or a relationship, it was just a vibe. But like, I was into it. He was in training, meetings, and physical therapy throughout the day and night. So, typically he called me late. When he called, we would talk for about five minutes before he fell asleep. It never failed. So, obviously, I was convinced that he called me just to hear my voice so that he can go to sleep. Ole Sappy Sally ass. The truth is that he's damn near narcoleptic; doesn't matter if he's mid-sentence, you are mid-sentence or if there's a whole damn party going on, Mark can fall asleep in the midst of anything.

One night, instead of going home to sleep, he came over. This was the third time we had spent real time together, second time since our initial meeting. We planned on just going right to bed. Like, instead of sleeping separately, we were just going to sleep together because I was sleeping when he called and he was sleepy, so why not? Naturally, we ended up having sex for the first time and it was pretty perfect. Remember I told you to stay focused? Forget that for a second so I can give you some details on our first time. Usually, I give way too many details, so since you and I just met, I'll try to scale back.

We started with simple touching. My hands were cold, his body was warm and his back was facing me. I just put my cold hands underneath his shirt, onto his warm back. His body tightened up and he turned around and hugged my body. While he hugged me, he rubbed his hands up the back of my shirt and asked me how my hands could be so cold if my body was so warm? I told him not to start a game he couldn't finish but he told me he finishes everything he starts. So he started. He grabbed my hand and placed it on his huge hard dick and simultaneously lifted my chin to his face to kiss me. I was wearing biker shorts and a tank top, so he just slid the shorts right off of me.

Then he entered himself into my vagina, but I felt him in my throat. He was inside of me, but somehow his body consumed mine. He was as deep inside of me as my body would allow. Whatever I could find on my bed to grip, I did. We were a perfect fit and it was great. After that, he could have had a key to the house, my social, the spare key to my car, I'll get an apartment in my name for him. Whatever zaddy wanted, he could have had it. Just kidding. Those were just penetration promises and they don't count. If you're wondering, the answer is no, we didn't use a condom — we were supposed to just go to sleep when he got there. The next day we woke up, I gave him a toothbrush. I got ready for work, he made a few business calls and then we sat on the couch and talked until it was time for me to head to the office. We walked out of my apartment together. When we were about to head to our cars, he grabbed me, complimented my hair. My hair at that time was super long and in a genie pony-tail on top of my head and laying over my shoulder.

H e gave me a kiss and then a hug and said, "What you doin' after work?"

I said, "I'm supposed to have drinks with the girls. Why? You wanna hang out with me?"

He laughed and kissed me again and said, "I might." His tone was sarcastic and playful.

I took a step closer to him, grabbed the front of his hoodie, and kissed him again. I started to walk away and while I did, I said, "Well, I *might* be available, call me later!" I gave him a promiscuous smile.

I didn't want to put too much on the night. I mean, it was great and I enjoyed every single second of it, but I knew that even though it felt so good, it was still so early. I knew I wasn't going to share much of that feeling with any of my friends. It felt different than anything else, so I wanted to keep it safe for as long as I could. When I say safe, I mean protecting the energy around that new situation in my life. Sometimes, we allow our friends and family into our relationships too soon and too deep, which I think gives them too much room for judgement and adds too many additional factors to the relationship.

Anyway, I did quietly inquire about him to a couple of the mutual friends we had. I just needed to know if what I was feeling was too good to be true. 'Cus you know sometimes we get ahead of ourselves. Especially when the D is good. But my friends were really here for a Mark and Kiana adventure. They all know me to be very picky and were so excited that this was the one I picked. Even though he asked for my number, I like to think that my game is tight and I pulled him, but he would remember the story differently. Either way, I told myself that I was going to fully live in every moment we shared.

We saw each other a few days later. It was a quick visit because I had time in between meetings and he had time in between his physical therapy session and his next meeting, so we met at my place. When we first met, we had already had a magnetic sexual energy between us, but after having sex for the first time, it was even stronger. Mark got to my place about five minutes after I got there and when he walked in, he greeted me with a kiss and gave me a long, tight hug.

Right away, he sat on the couch and made sure I sat right on his lap. We sat for a few minutes, each just talking about our day up until that point and then he stood us up and hugged me from behind while I was talking. It could just be around me, but Mark is secretly an antsy person. Like, he has to touch me or fidget with something all the time, it's very rare that he just sits still. Anyway, I led us to my bedroom because once he embraced me from behind, my pussy started to throb and I needed him.

When we got to my room, I turned around and looked at him and he said, "You know we don't have this kinda time."

I told him to kiss me and he did without question. I started to untie his sweats and pushed his body toward the bed and he never took his eyes from mine. This was only our second time being intimate, but each time, his dick got harder than I've ever felt a dick get before, which made me want him even more. I grabbed his dick out of his pants and used a little pressure to encourage him to sit down. He sat down, I dropped to my knees and immediately, he gathered all of my hair into a makeshift ponytail and held it there.

I fucking love when a man holds my hair without me having to ask him. I just feel like if you hold my hair on your own while I suck your dick, you deserve sloppy, soul snatching head every single time. He only allowed me to suck him off for about ninety seconds before he stopped me. He then stood me up, put his hand in my leggings and played with my clit for a few seconds before realizing she was already wet. He pulled my panties and leggings down at the same time, turned me around, grabbed my waist, leaned me forward and fucked me from behind.

When we were done, I went to the bathroom to freshen up and get myself together because I still had another meeting later that day. By the time I came out of the bathroom, he was already dressed and ready. I walked into the bedroom and he walked toward me with this unexplainable look in his eye. I guess the best way to explain it would be appreciation. Like, when he was looking at me, I felt like he appreciated my existence and I really loved that. We hugged when we finally met in the middle of the room and I told him we needed to get going so that we weren't late.

A s time went on, we became more consistent in each other's lives. Sleepovers became more of a regular thing, midday quickies happened more often and we really started to become really good friends too. That part was important to me because I've always believed that any strong relationship should have friendship as the foundation.

TWO

THE SWITCH UP

ONE DAY we were lying in bed and he told me that he was going to the Bahamas and then Miami to celebrate his friend's birthday. Not a big deal, live your best life, baby. You see, I encourage trips, outings, or whatever. I'm not the type of girl to be pressed or stressed if my man goes out without me. To be honest, I'm a homebody.

I'm the type of girlfriend that will feed and fuck you before you leave the house. I will be home cuddled up on the couch with the TV on for background noise while I enjoyed my group chats. Every now and again, I will step out with my man so that he can remember how fine I am when I get dolled up. Other than that, handle ya business, have fun, and don't have me out here looking stupid. The end.

. . .

The first day he was in the Bahamas, he posted a big group picture of all the travel buddies, which included rappers, athletes and lots of beautiful *Instagram* women. I wasn't concerned about any of the women. I was actually pretty confident in the foundation that we had been building. Up until that point, he didn't really strike me as the type of man to care about how many followers a woman had or how popular she was. He needed vibes. He needed good energy. He needed loyalty, safety, comfort, honesty, and purity. What he needed was me and you couldn't convince me that any of the women on that trip compared to me internally. Sure, some of them were beautiful with bomb bodies and thousands of followers, but they weren't me.

Besides that, the feelings associated with whatever him and I had been building were one of a kind. With that being said, I still wanted to see how he was gonna act. I mean, this was the first time since we had been dealing with each other that he had done something other than work. I was looking forward to seeing if he would still call or text me at any point throughout his trip. Somehow, I was going to utilize that information to determine how heavy he really messed with me. Looking back, it was probably a self-sabotaging move.

The entire Bahamas leg of this birthday tour was crickets. He didn't contact me one single time. I had even sent him a funny meme because like, how do you ignore that? He did though. Miami was up next and I was sure he'd finally reach out. Nothing. I wasn't hurt, but I was absolutely bothered. The Miami leg came to an end and he was finally back home. He had been gone for about two weeks. I knew when he had gotten home because ... research. So I was just waiting for him to tell me himself. It was the night after he had gotten home that he reached out. In a DM on *Instagram*. I couldn't believe it. As if he didn't have my number. "Yo. Don't be mad, I dropped my phone in the water the first night in the Bahamas, I haven't had a phone since." That's what he said to me.

Of course, Sappy Sally responded instead of Kilmonger Kiana. "Ok, I guess I'll stall you out," I replied. It was still questionable seeing as though he had posted two pictures during his trip. Lucky for him, the sap in me was grateful he at least reached out from his laptop. A few days went by without him having a phone. He would contact me via DM once or twice a day just to say hi or see how my day had gone and remind me that he hadn't gotten a new phone yet.

Eventually, he got a new phone and texted me. I think we had a brief text conversation that day and then spoke less the next day. I missed him. Not just physically, though. I felt a weird distance between us over the last few days and it didn't sit right with me. These were the types of things that caused me to do research. You see, I have this disgusting desire to understand the root of all things. Somehow, I've convinced myself that as long as I can understand the root of something, how I approach, accept or avoid putting myself in the situation turns out better in the long run. So, I needed to do research because I needed to know where the distance might have started before I brought it to his attention.

I started my research where we all start our research, *Instagram.* He had posted a picture with a female friend of his, who happened to be a pretty little *InstaModel* and they happened to be on the beach. When I saw the picture originally, I wasn't bothered at all. That's because we all know that if he's otherwise single and posts a girl on his page, he's not fucking her. So, I didn't even have an itch to research her page. I needed to look in his comments because if there was any girl in his life that felt any way about that, she was definitely going to leave something petty in the comments. Even if it was in code.

Brittany Vasquez didn't need code, she was a full production all on her own and everyone was going to know. Brittany was a child star but she still maintained a bit of her clout from that stardom. Of course, I did my own research on her and what I gathered was that although she was a beautiful girl, she suffered from insecurities. What it also looked like to me was that she didn't have many real friends. When I say real friends, it seemed as though all of her friendships were industry-based and fickle.

So, I figured she was the type of girl to build friendships with all of her man's friends and call them her own because the few friends she had weren't enough and she also seemed like the type to become best friends with her man's mom because of her lack of friendships and because that's how she would be able keep tabs. Those type of girls are annoying to me. With that being said, it seemed like the Internet was her opportunity to be who she wished she was, say the things she thought people would think were funny, and essentially overcompensate for who she really was, or wasn't. She isn't necessarily old, but it seemed like her spirit was and she was trying to keep it young. Obviously, this is all speculation, but that was the vibe I got from her.

Anyway, not only did she leave her petty comment, she tagged another girl so that they could have a full blown petty conversation together in the comments about the girl neither of them were bold enough to tag. That was my first piece of evidence that Mark Miller was switching up.

The next day, he texted me right before I headed into a meeting. I was already bent by what I had seen in the comments the day before, so I may or may not have been a brat from the jump. But whatever. He asked me how I was and my response was short. "Good. You?" Then I asked him if he would be sleeping in my bed that night and he said no. The audacity of me to have an attitude and still ask that is hilarious, but he never tells me no when I ask if he's sleeping over. He usually tells me it depends on this or that and then I send some pictures that'll encourage him to come over.

So when he told me no, I was offended. I told him I recognized the play he was running, because it was the same play I ran on men when I started my switch up.

The switch up typically happens when you've met someone else that you may be interested in, or you've gone back to someone you previously dealt with and you have to find a way to start weaning your current person off of what started to become the norm. Naturally, Mark said, "You trippin' over nothing. I didn't have a phone, I hit you from the computer when I could and I have been working. Ain't no switch up. What are you talking about?"

Honestly, he was right about all of it and I was probably being a psycho because I had started catching feelings for him.

They say if you look for dirt, you get dirty. So there I was, being a damn pedologist. The problem was that I hadn't asked any questions. I took what I saw and created the narrative I wanted to create. Well, it's not that I wanted to create it. It's just that I had already decided in my mind that this is what was happening, so it was downhill from there. Early in our relationship, well situationship, Mark had taught me a very valuable lesson. "If you have questions, you need to ask because the second you start assuming shit, you look crazy." I guess I had forgotten about that. I mean, it felt like it was right there in black and white but still, all of the things he was saying made sense too. I guess I just missed my dawg and the thought of another girl still thinking she had a spot really drove me nuts. That's how I knew I was really starting to like the guy. His crazy ass ex, or whatever she wanted to call herself, needed to let go. Beyond that, he needed to put her in her place, because yeah, she may very well be crazy, but a crazy bitch is really only as crazy as the nigga allows her to be. Fight me if you disagree.

THREE

SITUATIONSHIP

I THINK one of the trickiest parts of transitioning from situationship to relationship, is the conversation that clarifies the status. I think no matter how close you've become with your potential partner, it's an uncomfortable conversation to have. What if the other person was so comfortable with where the two of you stood, they don't want to move into the next step? What if this is just not the right timing for the other person? There's so many what ifs that can completely change the dynamic of what you've built up until that point. Granted, if conversation changes it for the worse, then better sooner than later, but it's still a tricky space.

Luckily, Mark had allowed me to be in my mood without tapping out of the whole situation all together.

He reassured me that he and Brittany were only friends. His exact words were, "Of course, I used to fuck with her. Brittany is crazy and all of her friends are petty. She told me she was going to do everything in her power to block me from dating anyone else and I told her I didn't care. She told me she would blow my comments up and I told her I would just erase it."

When he said those things to me, he wasn't defensive or upset, he just gave me the information. So I let it rock. I went through the pictures I had remembered seeing comments on and all of her nonsense was actually deleted, so I believed him. I had no reason not to and we picked right up where we left off before he went on that damn BahaMiami Birthday Tour. Oddly, I felt like that was us getting through our first real fight.

First fights are tough too. This is the first glimpse into who you are dealing with in an uncomfortable space. Which, I, personally, think is important in the getting to know you process. Really think about it, how well do you really know someone if you haven't gotten to see who they are when they're upset with you? That was a small fight, but Mark was patient, respectful, and fairly direct. These were all things that I could appreciate in a relationship. My ex was none of those things. He spewed fire at me. The worst things he could think of he would say them. The way that Mark handled an otherwise frustrating situation for a man, was almost refreshing. I'm not comparing them to one another, just acknowledging that there was a difference.

By that time, I had decided that any extracurricular

activity pertaining to men that I was involved with needed to stop. I needed to start pledging my allegiance. Whether or not he was ready, I had to start preparing myself for the possibility of it. I guess that sounds absurd, right? I mean, the idea of being loyal to a man who hasn't necessarily shown any loyalty to you is silly, isn't it? I didn't and still don't look at it that way, though. I'm a woman, that's how it's supposed to be.

At the time, I felt as though if he and I were ever going to take this to the next level, I didn't want to give any other men the room to say they had any part of me right before I became this or that with him. I guess for me, it was about respect more than it was about loyalty. The loyalty just came with the respect. I'm not the type of woman that would ever have my man out here looking crazy, even if he has me out here looking or feeling like a damn fool. I always stand strong in my beliefs and I work really hard at not allowing someone else's actions to alter my character.

After all, you don't need a whole circus to be a clown. Now, of course, I silently pledged my allegiance and I had no intentions of telling Mark that I dropped all my hoes until I knew for sure we were on the same page. He was very honest when asked the right questions. The issue is that in order to get the answers you were really looking for, you had to word your question in such a way that it covered all the bases of what you were actually asking. That's annoying. But since I knew that ahead of time, I had the ability to prepare. I wasn't falling in love yet, but I was walking to the ledge and needed to find some direction.

Against my better judgement, I knew I was going to ask Mark what we were doing. I played with the idea for a few weeks beforehand. I even spoke to one of my girls from the office about it. Not in detail of course, I just wanted an outsider's opinion on how they would approach the situation if they were in my shoes. Needless to say, she thought I should know what we were doing. If I'm honest, whether she agreed or not, I was going to do it. I knew my girls would be on the same page as me, but I still needed to feel justified. That's ego, not logic. Whatever the case, it was time to put my plan in motion. I didn't want him to feel cornered, pressured or overwhelmed. I just wanted to know where his mind was and if or how he viewed the future for us as a unit. I didn't even want or need to be an exclusive couple right then and there; it was literally just the comfort of knowing that our feelings were one thousand percent mutual.

S oon after I made my decision to find out what we were, he came over. When he got there, he was tired. I could tell he had a long day, so I figured I would hold off until the next morning to ask my questions. I just believe there's a time and place for every conversation, even more so when it's with a man. I won't lie, I was also a little nervous to have the conversation in the first place.

Anyway, he walked into my room and sat at the edge of my bed and just stared at me. I loved the way he looked at me. It was a very specific look. It gives me goose-bumps just thinking about it. It's like, in that moment, he needed me. He craved me. But not just physically. It's like his soul needed mine and even though he never told me when he had bad days, I could feel it in his energy. To this day, I don't know if he didn't tell me about his bad days because he was too prideful or if he didn't care enough to do so. I never pressed the issue, but I always felt it and whenever I did, I just made sure that my energy could protect his. I didn't and don't know what I was protecting him from, but something inside of me knew it was necessary.

He needed healing from something and I'm a healer. I needed to heal him. I wanted to be his safe haven even though I knew that he didn't completely trust me. He never said it, I just knew. With the pieces of him that he would give me, I could always feel the missing pieces. The thing is that I didn't think he was only hiding from me, I think he was hiding from everyone. There's nothing I could do to change that besides being me; open, honest and free of judgement whenever he was ready. That night, I stood in between his legs where he sat and just hugged him for a while.

Eventually, he took his shirt off, laid across the bed horizontally and I gave him a massage. He loved my massages. Sometimes, he didn't even need sex, he just needed his back rubbed or scratched until he fell asleep. My little baby. But I made sure that specific massage had a happy ending. Sloppy, sensual, soul-snatching head. Not only did I want to erase whatever day he had, I knew

I wanted to have 'the talk' when we woke up the next day, so I had to kill two birds with one stone.

The next morning, we woke up and had sex. After that, we just stayed in bed and talked about random things like we always did. Ironically, one of our conversations was about polygamy. We talked about whether a man wanted to partake in a polygamous relationship, he needed a pretty sturdy bag before he even presented the idea to his chosen women. Just so we are very clear, although I completely understand the concept of a polygamous relationship, I couldn't do it. But if I did, I'd have to be the first wife and I need to be the one that chooses all of the other women.

Anyway, it's like this conversation was the perfect intro to what I really wanted to discuss. So after we talked about how much money the man needed to have for this situation, I said, "Man, I just can't see myself willingly sharing my man". I was so nervous after I said it. I don't know if it was my nerves or my eagerness or both that caused me to just keep going, but I didn't stop. I rolled right into my question. "So, are we gonna play house forever? Or do you see us being exclusive at some point? I'm not saying right now, I'm just saying like, at some point in the future, do you see us being in an exclusive relationship?" There! I did it. I asked the question, which means I was going to get an answer, whether I liked what I heard or not, a response was coming. Mark is one of the smoothest men I've ever met. You barely know when he's uncomfortable or unprepared for a situation.

W ithout missing a beat, he replied, "I can't be in a relationship with anybody. I mean, I really just came out of a marriage. You know, it's crazy because I think a lot of times people rush into relationships because they feel pressured to do so. Women give men ultimatums and men just fall for it in fear of losing the woman. You gotta build friendships. You gotta know exactly who you're dealing with. I think that's why marriages don't last anymore. Because everybody rushes into situations they haven't fully assessed."

I was blown away. His reply was so well articulated. In that moment, it felt very honest. It was black and white, 'I can't be in a relationship with anybody'.

All I could say was, "That makes sense." I couldn't sit on the topic any longer than I already had. Truthfully, I needed to process it all. So, I changed the topic. I was, and still am, very good at changing the topic when I don't want to talk about the subject at hand. We woke up fairly early that morning because Mark is an early riser. Well, he was back then. It was very rare for him to sleep through the night. He was more of a nap throughout the day type of guy. During our conversation, he had asked me to scratch his back. I scratched it for him until he fell back asleep.

I always knew when he had fallen asleep because his breathing pattern would change. While I scratched his back, I began to process everything he had just talked about. I was very careful not allow the thoughts to consume me so much that they shifted my energy. As much as I could feel his energy, he could feel mine. As much of an overthinker as I was, so was he. With that being said, I processed his words.

You see, when I went into the topic of this conversation, I didn't expect him to tell me we should just make it exclusive right then and there. I didn't expect him to tell me anything that eluded to a confirmed commitment. On the other hand, I absolutely didn't expect him to tell me he couldn't be in a relationship, period! I'm not really sure what I expected. Honestly, until I sat there scratching his back, I thought I went into the conversation with no expectations at all.

Whatever I felt in that moment, said something different. I sat there, scratched his back and told myself that I needed to make sure I didn't become attached. I needed to ride it out for as long as I could without attachment because I really did enjoy his company, conversation, and energy. I enjoyed the vibe we had created, the otherwise unspoken understanding that we had, the fact that in the middle of the night, he would roll over and embrace my entire body right before he kissed me for no reason at all, not to mention the sex.

I really fucking loved our sex. It's literally like we fit perfectly for each other. He used to tell me I gave the best head he's ever had. Well, up until this very day, he tells me that I'm a legend. Ok, men will gas the hell out of you to get what they want, but when he would tell me that, I was super-gassed. Little ole me giving an NBA player, who has access to every baddie in the world, the best head he's ever had. That's lit! Sorry, I got sidetracked for a second.

Where were we? Oh, me wanting to ride it out. So, during that brief moment I had to quickly process it all, I decided that I would rock with him until I felt myself getting attached. When I say attached, I mean emotionally attached. Attached as in the thought of wanting to think and move like a unit. We already had these soul ties that neither of us had any control over, so I promised myself that if I felt myself losing control over my feelings, then I would walk away. I know it sounds irrational. If you're happy and it's working, why not just stay? The answer is simple, I was created to build a home, not just play house. Furthermore, if I walked away before I fell in love with him, then I would still be able to be his friend. You and me both know that niggas are good for ripping your heart to shreds, wiping your tears and then asking you if you could still be friends. I wanted to eliminate the shredded heart and the risk of losing lash extensions, but I also didn't want to lose my friend. If I allowed myself to fall in love with this man and he didn't fall with me, I knew I could never be his friend again.

Love is funny. I'm even funnier for thinking I would be able to control it. I mean, sure, I do believe that in order to find, feel and accept love in the romantic capacity, you must be open to it. But that wasn't the issue. I was open to it. Scared, but open. You see, although a number of men that I've dealt with would tell you different, I love hard. Really, really hard. When it comes to loving a partner, there is no gray area for me, I either love you wholeheartedly and unconditionally, or I don't feel anything for you at all. With Mark, so many things had already been different than any other situation I had been in. We didn't necessarily go through a talking or dating phase.

We sort of just jumped right in to a situationship. He cared about me. There was no doubt in my mind about that. I just felt like my feelings had been growing deeper than his and that was a scary thought for me. I told myself I would stay until I felt like I was becoming emotionally attached, so I did. But I started to pay a little more attention to how he acted after having that conversation. I think I just wanted to see if he would begin to take advantage of knowing where I stood or if he would start to pull back completely.

A fter we had *the talk* that morning, we stayed in bed for a little while longer while he slept and then it was time to get up and start our day. He needed to go to physical therapy and I had a meeting in the Hills. The talk didn't seem to throw off the energy like I thought it would. He didn't move any differently than he would have had we not had the talk, so I appreciated that. He left before me that day, so on his way out, he told me he'd call me later, gave me a kiss and I locked the door behind him. I had to have been in traffic for all of thirty minutes when he called me. I figured maybe he had left something at the apartment and needed to get back inside, so when I answered, I said, "What's wrong?"

He replied, "Nothing, I just wanted to talk to my dawg. You make it to your meeting yet?"

That was funny to me. Like, we just spent the night together, we just spent a majority of our morning together and we had just left the house maybe ten minutes apart from one another and there he was calling me like we hadn't spoken all day. That made me feel good.

From that day on, we absentmindedly began building a fairly solid foundation. Our sleepovers continued, our bond grew tighter, and our knowledge of each other grew deeper. One morning, we woke up and he had a meeting with a team that had been interested in signing him, so he was leaving before I did. When he attempted to leave, his car wouldn't start. It was obviously terrible timing but even worse, it was going to cost money that didn't need to be spent at that time. Initially, I didn't even know the car wasn't starting. It wasn't until about five minutes after he had been gone that he called me.

"Hi, love." I said with a smile when I answered because I thought this was just another one of his secret I miss you already moments.

He was clearly flustered on the other end of the phone. "Yo. This shit is crazy and I hate to ask you this, but can you drop me off at my meeting before you go to work? My fucking car won't start for whatever reason and I don't have time to wait for AAA or none of that. I'll figure out how to get to physical therapy from the meeting, I just can't be late to this meeting."

Man, I felt bad for him. He sounded so stressed out over the phone and I could tell that it was hard for him to even call me to ask for help. I didn't understand why though, like we were in that shit together, so we were certainly going to get through it together.

"You can just take my car. Stop stressing. I will call my job and tell them I need to work from home today."

Flustered, still, Mark tried to convince me not to call in. "Nah. You don't have to do all that. I just need—"

I cut him off, "Mark, it's fine. You can't miss this meeting. I am not going to lose my job for calling in one day. Plus, I'll still be working, I'm just going to do it from home. It's fine. Come get my keys before you make yourself late!"

I was standing at the door waiting for him when he walked up. He looked at me with so much gratitude and said, "Thank you. For real." He gave me two kisses before he left, one on the lips and then one on my forehead.

I didn't mind one bit. I knew that was such a stressful moment for him so later that afternoon, I walked to the hardware store near my house and got a key made for him. I knew maybe it was too soon for that, but I didn't like that he seemed to feel so uncomfortable asking me for help. The key was just going to be my secret until I felt like it was the right time, but I put it on my bulletin board in my room, so if he saw it, he saw it. At the time, his favorite snack was almonds and dried cranberries, so since I knew his day started rough and I didn't know what else would transpire between when he left and when he brought my car back, I grabbed those items for him too. Food always makes me feel better about life, so in my mind, it would make him feel better too.

He returned home...well, to my house a few hours later and had to get his car towed. Apparently, the starter went out. Before he hopped in the tow truck, I gave him the almonds and dried cranberries and he had a huge smile on his face.

L ater that night, we were on the phone and he said, "Hey, do you know how long it takes *Paypal* to send you one of those cards so that you can pull the money out immediately? I have a couple hundred dollars in my *Paypal* so I was just going to use that to pay for the car."

I didn't know the answer to that question but I had a solution. "Uhm, I'm not sure. But whatever you have on there, you can just send it to my *Paypal* and use my card. That way you don' t have to wait."

There was a sigh of relief on Mark's end. "Damn, you came through for me twice in one day. You are really my nigga."

We talked a while longer that night until Mark fell

asleep. Over the next few days, he was able to get the situation with his car handled and he was very happy about that.

We spent more and more time together. Our lives were pretty chaotic because we both had what seemed like a million things to do per day, but we were pretty good about sleeping in the same bed a few times a week. When we spent time together, it was so easy and natural. Mark is a super-affectionate guy, so each time he would walk in the house, he would greet me with a kiss and if it wasn't time to go to bed right when he got there, he was always very touchy-feely. When we slept at night, even if we didn't have sex, he would cuddle with me the majority of the night or sometimes just wake up in the middle of the night to kiss me.

We still hadn't been through any crazy trials or tribulations but we were building a really strong bond, which constantly took me back to that talk we had. When that conversation ended, I told myself that I would have to control my feelings and only stay in the situation until I couldn't handle it anymore. The more time we spent, the closer we were becoming. The more comfortable I got in operating as a unit with him, made it even harder to keep my feelings in check. At that point, I was ready to be with him officially. But I already knew how he felt about relationships.

FOUR

WALK.

I DON'T KNOW if I told you or not, but I'm a water sign. A Cancer. That means my emotions and feelings run incredibly deep, my thoughts travel fast and my moods are equivalent to an ocean tide. Sometimes, just waking up as a water sign is a struggle in itself. I hate to be cliché and say 'that's just who I am' but baaaaybee, that's just who the fuck I am. Today, for the most part, I have a pretty strong hold on my emotions. Back then, I was holding my emotions just as well as I could hold water in my hand. I think in the space we were in at the time, Mark was starting to get an idea of how I felt about him. He was a fool if he didn't. Like, I had 'the talk' with him so I imagine that would have been enough.

Oftentimes, men pretend to be oblivious to shit like

that, though. So I was starting to wonder if having had that conversation with him just went completely over his head or if he genuinely understood the space I was in. Even deeper than that, was he ever going to meet me halfway or were we just going to play house forever? It was starting to become more than I could handle. I was starting to have too much time to process things that didn't need to be processed and I was starting to comb through every conversation we had and every move he made.

None of these things were due to my lack of trust in him. I trusted him as much as you can trust a person who isn't actually yours, but I didn't and still don't know how to exist in a gray area. I craved and needed certainty. My desire to be both needed and wanted by a man is greater than my ability to exist in a space of what feels like constant transition. When it came to this situation or any situation, I needed it to be nothing other than black and white. The gut-wrenching truth was that this wasn't black or white and I was starting to feel like it was never going to be. That's when the fight or flight started to kick in for me because I was starting to feel too vulnerable and it was starting to feel too risky.

Being that Mark was part of the social circle he was a part of, celebrating birthdays usually meant a group trip rather than a one night event. He had told me on a phone conversation that he was heading to Miami with basically the same group from the Bahamas, but this time, it was for one of the girls' birthday. I always thought these little getaways were good for him. I felt like even if he wasn't sharing it with me, he was constantly stressed out. So I enjoyed the idea of him being able to get away from that and just live in the moment. I always feel like I was being sneaky, but I also felt like that trip was another good opportunity to see how he interacted with me while he was away, being that he had dropped his phone in the water during the BahaMiami shindig.

I know that it sounds so childish to place that type of secret pressure on somebody, but for whatever reason, it meant something to me. I was in a space of uncertainty. Well, not uncertain in my feelings at all, but incredibly uncertain in his. Some days, I would feel like he really cared about me. Other days, I would feel like he was just here because the sex was good. It wasn't that he was doing anything in particular that created this confusion, it was more or less the fact that I could feel such a void. I'm not afraid to admit that sometimes, I'm wrong. But I have never been wrong about how something or someone makes me feel. I needed something — anything that would help me lean more toward one or the other because if he wasn't going to take me out of that gray area, I was going to do it myself.

M ark wasn't much of a social media poster. Like I said, he posted things when he needed to, but not too much more outside of that. That being said, he was a bit harder to track through social media, so I would only see things here and there because I knew a few of the girls that were celebrating the birthday girl. The thing was that I wasn't even worried about whether or not he was booed up with anybody and I wasn't searching for anything, I was more concerned about if I would ever cross his mind enough for him to call me, drunk text me, anything. Initially, when he told me he was going to Miami, I didn't ask when he would be coming back or how long he would be gone. I think I just expected to still communicate with him while he was gone and I thought he'd be eager to see me, when he got back. I guess I was wrong. Well, I know I was wrong.

Miami was over and the squad was back in L.A. in a beach house. I had only known he was at a beach house because I saw him in someone else's *InstaStory*, which showed them at the beach house. That meant, an entire Miami trip had passed with him having no contact whatsoever with me. That didn't make sense to me. I also know that you're probably thinking, *bitch, why didn't you just hit him up?* That's not how things went for us though. He's always been the one that called me.

Although we both had hectic lives, his life moved at a lot faster pace than mine did, so it just always made sense that he would call me first thing in the morning or last thing at night. Occasionally, he would call me in the afternoon if he had a second, but those were few and far with bouts of texting sporadically throughout the day.

Whatever the case, we had an unspoken system and it seemed to be working for us.

B ack to what I was saying, Miami was over and he was back in L.A. He had been at the beach house for maybe twenty-four hours before I decided to reach out. I always tried to be considerate in my timing of things. I knew he'd be living his best life the entire time, but the real best life would be at night. So naturally, I hit him in the afternoon. I made sure my text was all-inclusive so that if I did get his attention, I kept it. "Hey, you. You back in L.A. yet?"

His three dots popped up almost instantly, "Yes, ma'am."

I was irritated with myself because I wasn't as all-inclusive as I wanted to be. I actually wasn't all-inclusive at all. I knew this already. You have to ask Mark very specific questions! He wasn't obligated to check in with me by any means, but he had sort of set that standard by doing so on his own so frequently. Regardless, he answered the question honestly, he just left out the part that he was an hour outside of L.A., at a beach house and was having too much fun to have even considered hitting my phone. Between me and you, as dramatic as it sounds, I told myself that if he didn't reach out to me at least once during this little getaway, I was definitely going to walk away. I had to.

· · ·

T hink about it, when he was home, we were damn near playing house and doing what couples do but still learning each other's minds; our souls had already seemed to have known each other. So why would being in a different time zone change his level of communication? I hate to say it, but I was starting to feel like I didn't actually hold a place in his heart. I was starting to feel like he was coming over because it was convenient and it was a safe place to get his dick wet. My feelings and my thoughts were all over the place at that point.

I had to respond, but with as little of the emotions that I was feeling as possible. "Oh, okay. Well if you need me, I'll be right over here." I kept it short and that was something we would say to the other when we missed them.

His three dots popped up instantly again, "Always need you."

You guys! I was losing my entire mind. His words didn't match his actions even a little bit. What he was saying to me was nowhere near how he was making me feel and it was starting to be too heavy for me. Up until that point, I hadn't told too many of my friends my concerns. I really just told them the good things about us. I try to stay away from sharing negative thoughts or feelings about intimate relationships because those are the thoughts and feelings that resonate more than anything positive when you tell them to people. You can tell a friend one bad thing about your relationship and then tell them three good things, but the only thing they will remember is that bad thing. I don't like that type of juju surrounding anything I'm a part of. With this though, I needed to just bounce my concerns off a few of my friends to see if I was being extra for no reason or with good reason.

F irst, I sent a text to one of my long time and logical friends, Kirsten. Kirsten is like the Timon to my Pumba, every single thing I am not, she is. Besides knowing me inside and out, she is one of the purest souls I know. She still believes in true love and she gives everybody the benefit of the doubt, even when they don't deserve as much. I always kept Kirsten as up to date as possible with my love life, but she always knew never to get too hyped about anybody I mentioned because it was usually only a matter of days before I didn't like him anymore.

Immediately after Mark sent his last text, I sent her a text that only said, "I think I have to walk away."

In true Kirsten fashion, she knew exactly what I was talking about, "Noooo! Why? What happened?

I knew she would be against it, I mean, last she heard, everything was going fine. So, I briefly told her my reasoning. "IDK, dude. I just don't like being in this gray area he has me in. He's been in Miami and now at a beach house and hasn't reached out to me one time. But beyond that, I'm starting to like him too much and he already told me he can't be in a relationship, so like, what am I doing here?"

She's so fair, "Ok, but like nothing has even changed negatively since that conversation, you're just being you and making it more complicated than it needs to be."

I hate that she knows me so well. "You don't know my life!" I don't know how to explain it, man. Something is just telling me I need to walk away before I don't even want to be his friend.

Being the ever so supportive friend that she is, but still keeping it real with me like she's supposed to, her response was brief, "I feel you and your intuition has never been wrong for as long as I've known you. At least sleep on it for a few days before you decide."

That was the thing. I had been thinking about it for the last two weeks. While we were getting closer, spending more time together, building what felt like a solid foundation, my feelings were growing stronger and my mind kept telling me I needed to slow down, but my heart didn't care. I wanted to ride it out for as long as I could, but I knew that if I continued to allow my feelings to grow, knowing that he wasn't going to grow in that same direction, I would despise him once he broke my heart.

Heartbreak was going to be inevitable, but I knew if walked away before I was in too deep, I would be able to salvage the friendship. If I walked away later, I wouldn't even be able to tolerate his existence. Kirsten's opinion mattered and to be honest, she was probably right about me making it more complicated than it needed to be, but I couldn't shake the feeling that I was justified in everything that I felt. I wanted the opinion of two more people that mattered to me. So I sent a group text to two of my best friends, Tatiana and Gianna.

Out of the three of us, Tatiana is the most logical, Gianna is basically the devil on your shoulder that tells you to do all the things you shouldn't do and I am the one that can see from both sides of the fence. Like I do with Kirsten, I keep both of them pretty updated on my love life. They knew pretty much every-thing up until this point. Our relationship is different than mine and Kirsten's, so their message was different. "Soooo, I guess I caught feelings or whatevaa and he ain't catching them back, so I'm pretty sure I gotta cut him loose...but I also miss him and I probably need to have sex with him one more time before I give him the boot."

Gianna responded first and she wasn't helpful at all, "LMAAAAAAAOOO! DEFINITELY GOTTA FUCK ONE LAST TIME!"

Tatiana was taking it a little more serious, but she still has no sense either. "LMAO! TRUUUUUE, TRUU-UUE. Are you mad he's at the beach house? Is that what brought this on?"

Man, the beach house was the least of my concern, "He definitely didn't tell me about that, but no. I don't even care about that. He said he can't be in a relationship pero like I feel myself heading that direction real quick so what's the point?"

Tati was on board, "Yeah, I feel you. We don't have

time to fall by ourselves. You think if you have sex again, it'll make it harder or easier?"

That question stumped me, "Honestly, IDK. I feel like either way, I'm in too deep."

Later that night, I was in bed, scrolling through my timeline, minding my gotdamn business. Mark posted a lil beach picture and guess who commented on it. If you guessed Brittany, you're right. She kept it real cute this time and just threw the wet emoji in his comments and he responded with an eggplant. I immediately took a screenshot and sent it to the group chat and then to Kirsten. I knew I was right. I knew I had all of those reservations for a reason. My intuition never lets me down. That was it for me. I didn't need any more confirmation.

I didn't need to sleep on it for a few days. I didn't need time to process anything else. The only thing I needed was to be done. My feelings were hurt. I felt like he lied to me, I felt used and above all, I was disappointed in him. I was disappointed because he tried to make me out to be crazy when I thought he and Brittany had something going on and he even made *her* out to be crazy. Even though the emojis didn't prove anything, they were enough to show me that he had been giving her enough to act like the crazy girl she had been acting like. She wasn't crazy, she had just been trolling her damn man that whole time. Son of a bitch.

I took a second to regroup and then I went to my notes in my phone to compose my farewell letter.

"Hi Mark Miller, I just want you to know that I think you are incredible. I think you're a King and nothing less. You know by now that I fuck with you. Heavy. When I asked you where you saw *us* going, you said that you couldn't be in relationship with anybody, and I respected and appreciated your honesty. I know myself and I know that sometime soon, that's what I'm going to want from you, so if I don't walk away now, my feelings are going to get hurt. I have to protect myself. So, this is me letting you know, that even though I don't want to, I have to walk away."

I must have read that message twenty times before I sent it. I was hurt and somehow, although necessary, it felt self-inflicted. So, after much hesitation, I copied the message from my notes and pasted it into his text thread and hit send. To be honest, knowing Mark the way I knew him, I didn't think he would respond immediately. I figured he was probably drunk and would need time to process what I had said, so I put my phone face down on my side table and tried to go to sleep as quickly as possible.

It took him all of five minutes to respond and his response was brief. "Ok, understood."

. . .

T hat was it. There was nothing to follow, there was no phone call after, it was the end of it. All I could do was take a deep breath and put my phone down. I knew Mark. I knew him well. Even though his response was short and less than empathetic, I knew he needed time to actually process what I had said. Beyond that, it was about eleven on a Friday night, in the summer and he was at a beach house; I'm sure he was drunk.

The following Monday, I was sitting in my office going through emails and enjoying a cup of black tea when my phone alerted me of a text message.

It was from Mark and it said, "How was your weekend?"

I had never been more confused by this man in the entire time I had known him. Before I responded, I sat there, dumbfounded and confused. I thought to myself, did he really just text me as if I didn't send an entire essay about having to walk away? Even more confusing is that he had never approached a conversation that way; like I couldn't think of one time in a million text messages and a hundred thousand phone calls where he asked me how my weekend was.

R eluctant, I responded with the same energy, "It was fine. How was yours?" Without missing a beat he wrote back twice in a row, "It was cool." "Miss you."

After reading that last one, I had to put my phone

down. I was so insanely confused. It didn't make sense to me why he was choosing to miss me *after* I had already walked away. I remember thinking to myself that he had to be insane because there is no way in hell he thinks it's appropriate to ignore the elephant in the room; hell, this was a whole zoo. Whatever the case, I was a sap then, I am a sap today and I will be a sap in forty more years too.

Sappy Sally had finally mustered up the energy to respond. "Miss you too." As soon as I hit send, I had wished I had more strength than that.

I was sort of disappointed in myself, you know? Why couldn't I have just called him out on his lack of accountability? Why couldn't I have addressed the topic I felt needed to be addressed? Why did I just let him sweep what mattered to me under the rug? I didn't know the answers to those questions then and I still don't know the answers now.

He waited a few minutes before sending his next text, "WYD tomorrow?"

I thought he was starting to be facetious and that was frustrating too. "You know my life, Mark Miller."

I think he could feel my frustration because he stopped bullshitting and got straight to the point. "I rented a gym for tomorrow so that I can shoot around for a few hours, will you come help me stretch and rebound my shots?"

I couldn't believe him. For as long as I had known him, for as much time as we had spent, as often as we spoke, he had never invited me into his world. It's almost like he intentionally kept me separate from his basketball life and I didn't even realize I was affected by that until that very moment. I didn't know if my emotions were just on a wild roller-coaster or if I was starting to find the clarity I had been searching for all along. At the same time, it warmed my little heart that he invited me. Part of me felt like maybe this is his way of fighting for us and still keeping his pride intact in the process. Mark was just as analytical as I was. So, I knew there had to be a method of some sort to his madness, I just wasn't sure what it was or why he was choosing now to show this side of him. While I was trying to process what was happening, he called me.

F or whatever reason, my heart was racing and my palms were sweaty when I answered. "Hey." I have no idea what I was so nervous about.

He was slightly aggressive on the other end of the phone, more aggressive than I had been used to. "I know you read my last text."

That was a little funny to me because honestly, it had to have been all of five minutes between him sending the text and calling me. He knew I was at work, so the fact that he was so impatient that he decided to pick up the phone and press me was a little bit of a turn on. I like when niggas that I like press me. Now, if he was a nigga that I didn't like and he was just on the roster because there was an open slot, there's no way in hell he could have pressed me and gotten away with it. But coming from Mark, I liked it. It almost made me feel like he felt a little pressure to step up. I never doubted that he knew my worth, but I was certain he didn't understand my value and maybe he was starting to get a vague idea of it when I was on my way out.

I chuckled a little when I responded, "I did. I'm working, so I just hadn't had a chance to respond just yet. What time do you plan on going? I suppose I can try to make it. I mean, I'm not a professional stretch coach and I am certainly not going to rebound any shots because I won't be sweating my edges out for you. But if a ball rolls my way, I guess I could roll it back to you."

He patiently listened to my entire fake speech before he responded, "You know, you talk a lot of shit. All you had to do was ask what time and tell me if you were going to come or not. But I have the gym from noon to ten at night, so come whenever."

I was relieved that we were able to remove some of the tension. "Yeah, well that would have been too easy. But alright, just text me the address. I'll probably just come at one o'clock because I have other stuff to do."

I didn't have anything else to do that day other than happy hour with my girls and to be honest, if I would have cancelled on them for some dick, neither of them would have questioned it. I just needed to redeem myself from being weak so early on. I know that I had chosen to walk away, but I figured if he was asking me to come to his workout session, which he had never done before, he was trying to tell or show me something. I cared about him so I was willing to listen to or see whatever it was.

The next day, I showed up to the gym in North Hollywood at one o'clock, like I said I would. When I walked in, he gave me a tight hug; he was so happy to see me. A friend of his was sitting on the sidelines, so he briefly introduced me to him. It happened to be his cousin, Hoov, not his friend and this was funny to me. That whole time I had been dealing with Mark, I had never met any of his friends. He would have full phone conversations with them while I sat right next to him and he would talk to me about them as if I had known all of them for years, but I never met them.

The crazy thing about it was that this was another moment where I hadn't realized I was affected by it until it was placed right in front of me. Even though I missed him and even though I was so happy to see his fine ass, I was starting to think that maybe I had made the right choice. I was starting to feel like I didn't actually know him as well as I thought I did. I knew him as well as he wanted me to. That led me to frustration. Mind you, all of this was internal and quick. But, at that moment, I was sure I made the right choice. I mean, curiosity killed the cat, so I didn't leave, but I was definitely feeling like I was right.

.   .   .

W e all sat down on the sideline chairs and Mark looked at me and smiled. "Kiana. You really my nigga, man." Still cheesing from ear to ear, "You didn't even give me a hug when you came in here. You came in here looking all sexy. You did that for me, huh? Give me a Mark and Kiana hug. Hug me like you hug me when I pull up to the house."

I was smiling like a fool. But I was puzzled inside because I knew there had to be a reason for all of this and I also knew for a fact that I hugged him when I walked in. My confusion was making me bounce my leg while I sat there but my joy to see him was causing me to fall right into his trap. "First of all, knock it off. I told you I had stuff to do after this, so I just dressed for both occasions. You're just not used to seeing me dressed because you keep me in the house. Secondly, I absolutely gave you a hug as soon as I walked in here. When have I ever greeted you without a hug? You just disregarded it. Stand up, so I can give you another one."

H e sat there with a smile on his face, looked over at Hoov while he stood up from his chair and said, "Hoov, you see how she treats me, man?"

We all laughed as Mark embraced my body. I was wearing a casual mini dress, a jean jacket and some chucks. When he hugged me, he hugged inside of the jacket and his arms could basically wrap around my small body twice if he would have squeezed me any tighter. He rubbed all over my back and grabbed my ass. I missed him so much and I knew I was going to miss him even more by the time that entire visit was over. We sat back down and Mark just stared at me as if he had never seen me before. I don't know if he was happy to see me or sad that he knew I was leaving.

He looked over at Hoov, who was just minding his business while he played on his phone. "Hoov, did I tell you Ki broke up with me, man?"

I was fucking floored. I couldn't believe he had just said that, yet alone, said it out of the blue. I gasped and clutched my imaginary pearls.

"Hoov, don't let him scam you. We weren't even together." I shot a death stare back at Mark.

Just then, another friend of his walks into the gym. Zeke. Never met him either and this couldn't be a worse time to meet the whole damn squad. Mark introduced me to Zeke and then they both sat down.

Hoov waited until everybody was sitting before he picked up right where we left off. "Kiana, I'm gonna tell you like this. You are a beautiful girl, stand your ground." Hoov gave me all the OG vibes. His energy was magnetic and you could tell that his spirit was pure. I liked him because I could tell he was the type to keep it real, no matter what.

· · ·

Mark was fake offended. "Hoov. Nigga. Whose side are you on?"

I was really offended. I couldn't believe Mark would ever bring that up in that moment. I didn't even hold my breath when I started talking, "Hoov, you don't have to choose sides. But, if you were working a job that you really liked but you weren't being paid for it and you were doing everything right and then you asked the manager when you were going to start receiving payment for your work and he said you won't receive payment; would you quit the job or continue to work for free?"

Hoov looked at me and started nodding his head in agreement. Before he could even open his mouth to speak, Mark stood up and interrupted. "First of all, great fucking analogy." Then he continued to walk toward Hoov so that he could get his defense off.

Hoov cut in to agree with Mark. "Incredible analogy. I don't even need to hear more. I don't even know what the analogy is in reference to, but I'm not working for free and you should never work for free either. No matter how much you like the job."

Mark was at ten now. "Hoov! No! I wasn't even accepting applications! Her resume came across my desk and it was A-1."

I didn't let him finish, "You weren't accepting

applications and I wasn't applying but you still took my resume and hired me!"

At that point, Mark was walking back towards me, visibly frustrated. "I would've been a fool not to! Do you know what your resume looks like?"

I admit, I was flattered but he was irritating me. I was sitting on the edge of my seat, so I leaned back, rolled my eyes, crossed my arms and pouted like a child. "Of course, I know. I typed it up."

The energy in the room was so weird that day, but as I sit here reminiscing, it was really funny. I don't even know why Mark decided to bring up our issues at that moment or in that way. I just felt like there were so many other ways to go about the situation. I also really resented that he chose the first time I met anybody in his life to do it. What a fucking awkward first impression.

Anyway, Mark was bothered too, and he's the one that started this nonsense. "Yo, Hoov. Can you go buy me a bottle of *Ciroc* for tonight? Zeke, go with him. 'Cus we need the gym so we can talk."

I'm childish, so this was inappropriately funny to me, but I laughed and tried to convince Hoov to let me go with them. "Hoov, maybe you need an extra set of hands. I don't wanna be in trouble in here by myself." I chuckled.

Hoov stood up, looked me dead in the face and said, "Listen, I don't know the whole story or any of it, really but I'mma tell you this – stand your ground. You don't have to take his shit and I don't care that he's my cousin. You don't take anybody's shit and you make sure your voice is heard. Choose your battles wisely. You don't have to win every battle to win the war."

I listened to him and took what he said to me right to the heart. I only met him that day, but I appreciated him for that. He didn't know what was going on between Mark and me, but somehow, in the little time that we had to exchange energy, I felt like he understood my value. He and Zeke both walked out of the gym. I just sat there with my head down. I was a lot of things in that moment. I was upset because he chose the worst time possible to discuss what he could have discussed three days prior. I was embarrassed because I had never met any of his friends before that moment and that was going to be their only impression of me. I was hurt for all of the same reasons.

Mark sat down in the chair directly across from me. "You really just tried to play me in front of everybody."

Bitch, I was really blown. I couldn't believe he had just opened his mouth to say that to me. I looked up at him without even lifting my head, reminding myself not to cry. "Are you kidding? Get real. You brought that up. I never would have considered having that conversation in front of anybody else."

He was agitated. Some nerve. He rubbed the waves on his head and tried to change his approach. His tone was different and he leaned forward in his chair with his elbows on his legs. "I never said I couldn't be in a relationship."

I was still very annoyed, but I appreciated the slight change in his tone. I lifted my head and looked at him and tried to lower my guard a bit. "Mark, I didn't make that up. By now, you know that I remember ninety-eight percent of our conversations verbatim. I never would have walked away if you hadn't said that. So, don't do that."

He started to get agitated again, but I didn't understand why. I was calm. My energy was calm. He was just bothered, I guess. "Well, you're naive if you thought I meant forever. Who wants to be single forever?" He got out of his seat, walked to the wall next to me, leaned against it, put his hands in his basketball shorts and stared at me. "Do you understand that when I met you, I had just come out of a marriage? My wife woke up one day and just decided she was done. It's like she had an epiphany and that was it for her. All I took was my car. I left everything; the house, all my TVs, everything. Up until two months ago, I was still paying the mortgage on that house! I have abandonment issues and you fucking left. Out of nowhere, you basically woke up and decided to leave. You know how many of my niggas I have lost to jail, to the streets? Over money? So when I read your message, it was just like, 'alright, cool. Another one bites the dust.' I am nowhere near ready to be in a relationship. If I meet somebody and she knows how to be my friend first and she makes it clear she ain't going nowhere, I'll sign some fucking papers again. But I'm broken right now. I don't even know which way is up from down. I lost my family, but I lost my whole fucking career before that. If I'm going to be with somebody, I gotta be prepared to take on everything she has too. I can barely run my own life right now. How am I supposed to take care of you too? I thought we were good. Like, I really thought we were building a foundation. It was me and you, there was no other bitches; it was just us. I was giving you everything I had to give you and obviously that wasn't enough for you."

The entire time he was spilling his heart out to me, he never broke eye contact. He never took his eyes from mine and I never took mine from his. That moment was the most transparent moment he had ever given me. That was the piece of him I constantly felt like I was missing. That was the part of him that he was hiding from me and the part of him that I wanted to heal but didn't know existed. When I had walked into the gym that day, I was certain that I had made the right decision. But after that moment, after he spilled his heart out to me, I wished I would have been a little less fearful of being hurt, so that I could have waited a little longer for him to come around.

I was protecting myself. I had endured so much pain from my last relationship and muscled through so much disappointment from people I had considered family in the past, that I wanted to prevent this story from being the same. We had never spoken in detail about his divorce or his marriage, for that matter. The few times we had spoken about it, it seemed as though he had already dealt with the pain portion of it, so I never probed. I was sorry that I didn't because maybe I could have helped him heal through it. It's not like I had ever been married before, but I could have provided a safe place for him to go through the different emotions he needed to feel in order to heal. I felt so many things in that moment. I wanted to hug him and sock him in his shit at the same time. I wanted to hug him, for obvious reasons. I wanted to sock him. Why didn't he open up sooner? Why didn't he just tell me he was too hurt to consider a relationship when I asked him about it? Why did he make his answer so permanent?

I sat there, reminding myself not to cry and trying to choose my words carefully. "I'm sorry." I wasn't sure if I should just stop there or explain myself. I wanted to just stop there and let that be my response. I couldn't. "I didn't abandon you though. I told you I was walking away. I told you why I was walking away. And, I told you that I was still able to be your friend. I didn't just disappear out of your life. I'm sitting in the gym with you right now. I responded to your text messages. I didn't abandon you. I never would have walked away if I knew you didn't mean forever. I'm far from naive. If a man tells me he cannot be in a relationship, then who am I to believe anything different.

I would be a fool to think I could change a man's

mind. I didn't want to give you the opportunity to hurt me to my point of no return. I am all I have. Who will protect me if I don't protect me?" My voice was starting to crack as I fought back tears. "This is the most transparent you've ever been with me. I think I learned more about you right now than I've learned in our entire existence. That doesn't make sense to me. We sleep in the same bed. We share so many things. You're telling me that it was just us, but you were never mine."

He cut me off. "I was definitely yours."

I cut in just as quickly as he did. "But you weren't. You were never mine. I watch Brittany Vasquez check you in your comments like she's your girl on a regular basis. So, you don't get to tell me you were mine. You don't get to tell me it was just us."

He was agitated again. "Man, Brittany and I used to deal with each other. It didn't work out and we are still friends. Brittany is crazy and all of her friends are petty. I already told you that she told me a while ago that if she couldn't have me, no one would and that she would make sure of it. So, it was just us. And you walked away."

I had a lot to say to that. I had a lot more questions about it. I didn't want to fight anymore though. That visit was exhausting and I hadn't even cried. I knew that I wanted to continue to build though, so I just tried to move forward. "I'm sorry I walked away. Can we keep building? Can we pick up where we left off and vow for complete transparency moving forward?"

He looked at me and then turned his head away and shook it. "You left man. I don't trust you anymore."

Those words cut me deep. I felt like I was punched in the chest and I needed to catch my breath. I was on the verge of tears at that point, but I needed clarification before I jumped to the conclusion I thought he was at. "You don't trust me? How do you not trust me? So, that's it then? The answer is no? We can't keep building?" So much for jumping to conclusions, I didn't even breathe in between asking those questions.

He rubbed his waves again. That's what he does when he is uncomfortable. "There's different levels to trust. I still trust you as a friend, but I no longer trust you as a romantic partner. So, that's not it as far as our friendship goes, shorty. But it's a wrap for anything else."

My eyes filled up with tears, so I put my head down, started grabbing my purse and the water bottle I walked in with and made my way toward the door.

He followed after me. "Kiana."

I didn't stop. I kept walking until I was outside of the gym. I thought the he had stopped following me, but since he's so damn tall, three of my steps equal one of his. As I turned to make sure the door closed behind me, he was right at the door. Luckily, my tears had gone away for a moment.

"You're just going to walk away after I called your name?"

I couldn't even look him in the face at that point. I kept my head down and my voice was cracking when I opened my mouth to talk. "For what? So you can see me cry? I'm good. You win." I walked away.

W hen I got into my car, I sat there with only the sound of my crying. Usually in situations like that, my thoughts are loud, but in this situation, it's like my brain was empty and my heart was full of pain. I didn't regret my decision to walk away, but I meant my apology when I said it. Prior to having that incredibly transparent conversation in the gym, I had no idea that he cared about me that much or that I even had the power to remotely hurt his feelings. I didn't agree with his feeling of abandonment but my actions made him feel that way and he's not wrong for feeling how he felt. Who would I be to tell him 'your feelings are wrong'. That's absurd. I finally pulled myself together enough to start my car and drive home and I cried all the way there.

I genuinely felt like I was justified in walking away but on the other hand, I felt like it was my responsibility to fight for what I wanted. When I got home, I took my shoes, jacket and dress off. I left them right where I stood and climbed into bed. I just needed to sleep. I don't know if you know, but a real good heartbreak cry is fucking exhausting. It'll take every ounce of energy and strength you have and then pull from the reserve energy and take that too. I was lying in bed on my back, with the comforter pulled all the way up to my chin, looking at the ceiling with tears streaming down the sides of my face and into my ears.

I'm dramatic, so I put Mariah Carey's 'Mine Again' on repeat and balled my eyes out. By the third time it played, I didn't have any more tears to cry so I started singing. Singing isn't one of the talents God felt was necessary for me, so I started laughing at myself and how terrible I sounded. Then I realized how dramatic I was being by listening to a song that made me cry more than I was already crying. I told myself to get a grip. I don't think I really had a choice. My mind was in overdrive, my heart was broken, my head was pounding, my emotions were all over the place. I was cry-singing a song well out of my range. I remember thinking to myself, *This man is driving me crazy. How did I let it get here?*

I had finally fallen asleep after that. I had woken up at two-thirty that morning with a heavy heart. I was replaying the part when I asked Mark if we could pick up where we left off and he said no. I knew him well enough to know that he meant it, but I had to get what was in my heart off, even if it didn't change his mind.

I grabbed my phone, opened my notes and began to type my heart out.

I'm sorry for walking away today, but it's not in my character to let a man see me cry. Today is the most honest you've ever been with me and I wish you would have done that sooner. I never would have walked away if I had already known some of the things you said today.

But I guess that doesn't matter now. You have to let someone love you, Mark. You can't hide forever. You have dark places inside of you, but your dark places don't mean you are undeserving of love. You are a king regardless of what you've been through. I know that you don't trust me anymore, and that makes me sad, but I hope you know that I'm here. And I'm patient. I'm the most patient and understanding person you will ever meet. If you need to sit on my couch and cry, I'll wipe your tears. If you just need to get shit off, I'll listen. I could have even been patient through your healing process if I had known you didn't mean 'forever'. But you can't push everybody away that wants to love you just because you're hurt. It's not fair. I wanna grow with you. I wanna help you heal, if you let me.

He never responded.

FIVE

ALWAYS RIGHT

WALKING AWAY from my situation with Mark was hard. Honestly, it was devastating. We had such an incredible bond and it was so incredibly organic that I knew it'd be hard to find that so seamlessly with anyone else. It's so rare that I allow a man into my space physically, but especially emotionally, and I was willing to let Mark move into my space. Literally.

Two days later, I was lying in bed sulking in my sorrows. I know that sounds like I was being extra, but in order for me to heal through things, I have to allow myself to feel them entirely. Otherwise, I continue to relive the moments that caused me pain and harbor those feelings. With that being said, not only was I sulking, I had called the office to let them know I was going to work from home so that I could sulk peacefully. I don't know if he needed time to process the fact that I walked away, reconsider my question of picking up where we left off or if he just missed me, but my phone rang and it was him.

My heart dropped and my voice was shaky but I tried to keep it together. "Hi, Mr. Miller." My tone was somber.

Whether it was intentional or coincidence, his energy matched mine and he was somber too.

In a stern but somber voice, he said, "What's up, shorty? How you?"

I sat up in my bed before I responded, "I'm okay. How are you?"

I don't think he really cared what I said, he was just waiting for me to stop talking so that he could start.

He started talking way faster than I was prepared to listen. "I'm cool. You know, obviously, I read your essay the other day and the way you talk to people is craaaazy. Like, you just say whatever the fuck you want with no regard to respect."

I was completely shocked by this information. Literally – mouth open, eyes wide, eyebrows raised – at a loss for words.

He continued, "Niggas literally get killed in the streets for lack of respect. I'm one thousand percent sure that disrespect wasn't your intention, but intent does not matter. If you standing next to the nigga I intended on shooting, but I shot you instead, my intent don't matter. The only thing that matters is that *you* were the one that was shot."

I sat quietly, but in my mind, I was thinking, *well that escalated quickly.*

Bishop Miller kept going. "You wanted to tell me about myself so bad that you didn't even give a fuck about your delivery. My daughter's mom came from a domineering matriarch. She would say any and everything she wanted to say to me. All her family members speak to their niggas and people around them however the fuck they want. I cannot stand that and I told myself when we were done that I would never settle for anybody that carried those characteristics. That's not the type of woman I would ever be with. Period."

Offended was an understatement. So, whatever you can feel that's worse than offended, that's what I felt.

I wasted no time responding. "That's deep. If you want to be technical, in regard to intent, if you accidentally hit somebody with your car as opposed to intentionally hitting somebody with your car, your sentence would be different. So, although intent may be irrelevant here, your analogy was pretty far out. Maybe my delivery was flawed, but I don't believe the message was at all disrespectful. So, I'm sorry that you received it that way. When I was growing up, my mother always talked at me rather than to me to get her point across, so maybe I projected that in my message. In which case, I'm sorry. I hated that feeling and would never want to make anyone else feel that way.

I do, however, believe that for you to sit here and tell me that it would be *settling* for you to choose me, is disrespectful. I've done nothing but treat you like a king for as long as I've known you, so that's a low blow. You have a way of making me feel like I'm not enough for you, no matter how hard I try and my mom used to do that to me too. Maybe it's a Virgo thing. But it's interesting that I would sit here and fight for you to stay when I don't even feel like enough. So, if your goal was to be as disrespectful as you felt I was, you got it."

I wasn't trying to play victim but I damn sure wasn't going to sit quietly while I felt like he was trying to belittle me. I didn't know if my essay had struck a nerve or if I was so far off that it pissed him off, whatever the case, his return speech was just as flawed as he felt the delivery of my essay was and he needed to know that. Respect is reciprocated. The fuck!

His tone softened and he pulled back a bit. "Nah, shorty, you misunderstood what I said. I think you're a queen. I love our conversations. I love that we can just lay in the bed for hours and talk about everything. I love spending time with you. I love your point of view on things. You're a great cook. You're smart as hell. You always smell good. The head is fire. The pussy is great. All of that. But you drew a line. I was really rocking with you. It was really just us, regardless of what you think. I understand your reasoning for walking away, I just can't do lines. I have abandonment issues and that makes me feel abandoned. You don't think I miss you already? If we weren't like this, I'd be at your place, inside of you for the second time already. I need my back scratched. I need a Kiana hug. But you drew a line, shorty."

It was just like him to say all the things I needed to hear when I really wanted to punch him in his shit. His charm was almost manipulative. He should have been a rapper instead of an athlete the way he was always able to play his words. Even still, how could he keep telling me he was mine, when I didn't feel like that?

It's silly to have asked this question at that point in time, but I was curious. "If it was just us, why do I feel like I'm your best kept secret? Like, your best friend lives down the street from me and you've never introduced me to him. I have never met any of your friends, with the exception of Hoov and Zeke the other day, and that was by accident. You've been telling me for months that you would let me come sit in on a workout and you never did until I walked away. You keep me out of such a huge part of your life and I don't understand why."

By now, you know this nigga never misses a beat. Even if he isn't prepared, he has an answer for everything that can or will be said and you would never know he wasn't ready. He's quick. It's dangerous. The other side of that, is me. I can feel energy like no other. It doesn't matter if I'm texting a person, talking on the phone with them, or standing right in front of them, I can always feel a shift in moods and energy. When I feel the shift, I'm always sure to protect my energy from shifting so that I can fully receive the energy the other person is emitting. With that being said, I knew Mark was about to pull an answer out of his ass and I knew I was just going to let him. It's chess. I'm always playing chess, so I'm always making sure the queen is protected; even at my weakest.

Like I expected, his energy shifted the second he opened his mouth. "Ok, first of all, I knew Hoov and Zeke we're pulling up to the gym, I just didn't know what time, so it wasn't an accident that you met them. Which would mean you're not my best kept secret. You're not a secret at all. Those are two of my closest niggas and you just met them. My family lives almost two hours away and you know that. So, with your schedule, when is it ever really a good time for you to drive all the way out there to meet them? Like, that's so far out of the way, it's crazy. And I for sure don't keep you out of any parts of my life. I talk to you about training all the time. I been meaning to have you come sit in on a workout and when you walked away, that was the right time, in my opinion, because I needed to know if we were still friends and you showed up because you're a real one."

Mark is fucking annoying. I was annoyed to my core. His answer was bullshit and I was tired.

I didn't even want to debate him, so I just said "Okay, Mark."

He knew I thought he was full of shit, so he turned the charm up a little more. "Can I come over for one last hug? Or is that totally out of the question?"

I closed my eyes because my thoughts were so loud, I needed to refocus. As I closed my eyes, it's like I saw my thoughts in writing instead. *Who does this man think he is? Why does he think that's appropriate? When will he ever stop being SO confusing? What is my problem?*

My problem was that I said, "Yes, you can come get one more hug, one time for the one time." I rolled my eyes through the entire sentence, as if that changed the fact that I was saying yes.

I didn't even bother pulling myself together too

much, because I was an emotional wreck. All I had on was a T-shirt and panties. It wasn't like he hadn't seen me naked before, so I didn't even care to put clothes on. Honestly, I didn't even have the energy. It had only taken him about thirty minutes to get to my place. When I opened the door, we both just stood there and looked at each other for a second before he walked in. Seeing him filled my heart with so much joy and so much pain at the same time. I was constantly conflicted when it came to him. I walked backwards as I opened the door more and left room for him to walk inside. He still stood there for a second. I'm not sure what we were doing.

I was standing with one hand on the door knob with my head leaned against the door, looking him dead in his eye. He was standing in the doorway, leaned against the opening with his hands in front of him and one foot crossed over the other, looking right back at me. When he finally walked in, I moved away from the door and he closed it behind him, walked toward me, and squatted down a bit so that he could hug me from my waist. We didn't even say a word to each other for the first maybe thirty seconds of the hug. I am being literal when I say first thirty seconds because we hugged for at least forty-five seconds. Then, he picked me up, I wrapped my legs around his body and he led us to my bedroom. Still without saying a word, he leaned forward and gently placed me on the bed, stared me in my eyes and bit his bottom lip while he took my panties off. His dick was rock hard and my vagina was slippery wet. He pulled me toward the edge of the bed, grabbed both my hands, interlocked our fingers, lifted my arms above my head and guided himself inside of me.

His dick was so hard, he didn't even need to use his hands. He started slow. It was like we both knew this was the last time, so it felt different. The emotions were different and the energy was new. Maybe three minutes in, he started fucking me hard, really hard. That was different too. It wasn't like he was angry, it was more like he had a point to prove. I don't know what that point was, but it almost felt territorial, like he needed to remind himself that this pussy was his and was going to continue to be his. When it was time, he pulled out, used his right hand to grab and shake himself as his left hand gripped my thigh tightly while he came on me. He walked into the bathroom and came out with a warm towel to clean his juice off of me.

I had to break the silence because it was killing me. "Well, at least you're still a gentlemen."

He laughed and snapped out of whatever trance he was in and replied, "I almost nutted inside of you."

I rolled over halfway so that my vagina wasn't just in the air anymore and nonchalantly said, "You should have, that's why I went on birth control anyway."

We laid in my bed for about an hour, mostly in silence, while I traced different parts of his body with my fingers. Eventually, he started to gather his things and I knew that it was about to be the end for real. I stood on the bed like I always did, so that I could be taller than him when I hugged him. I tried to kiss him and he moved back slightly and then flicked my bottom lip like he always did.

Slightly offended, eyebrows twisted, I called him out on it. "You better kiss me."

We hadn't kissed the entire time he was there and I hadn't noticed until that moment when I attempted to kiss him.

He stood there and played with my bottom lip and his eyes toggled between looking at my lip and looking in my eyes when he said, "We can't kiss. You walked away from me. You abandoned me. I know you're going to have a lot to say about that, but I have to go. So, I'm giving you thirty minutes after I leave to send your essay. If you don't send it within thirty minutes, I am not going to respond to it."

I just stared at him. It was such a blow to my gut that I felt like I could barely breathe.

With a sympathetic smirk on his face, he said, "Don't give me that look. Come walk me out."

I just rolled my eyes and looked away. I tried my best not to let a tear fall down my face.

We walked to the front door, him in front and me behind a few steps. I walked with my head down. I don't know why, but I felt so insecure in that moment. When we got to the door, he opened it slightly and then turned around and looked at me. I looked up at him, reminding myself to be strong, don't cry, and keep your head high. I had so much to say, but I knew the second I opened my mouth, tears would come streaming down my face quicker than I could control them.

He grabbed at my waist and pulled me closer to him. "Gimme a hug, shorty. I'll hit you later."

I stood on my tippy toes, grabbed the back of his neck with one hand and pulled him in with my other arm and gave him the tightest hug I could muscle. My heart was racing. I'm sure he could feel it from my body through his. My breathing was labored and confusing so I tried to get my pattern to just fall in line with his so that I could find control. That was it. We unraveled our bodies and he walked out. I closed the door behind him and locked it. I could finally breathe. I finally cried. I leaned my back against the door, interlocked my fingers, placed them above my head, looked up at the ceiling and tears rolled down my face into my ears and down my neck. I couldn't believe any of that had just happened. I slid my body down the door, sat there and cried for as long as my body could produce tears. Once I was done crying, I had to take a warm bath with Epsom salt. Whatever point Mark was trying to prove, left my pussy lips swollen and achy.

A few days had gone by and I was finally starting to feel like a human again. That first couple of days were taxing. I did everything I was supposed to do as a functioning adult, I just didn't remember having done it. Every single day, it was like I had driven from one destination to another without knowing if I had actually stopped at any red lights. Fortunately, I guess, I was moving out of devastating pain and transitioning into anger. I was starting to remember who the fuck I was and who I was going to be. I reminded myself that before this nigga, I could have had any man I had access to.

I questioned my pain because I was frustrated with the fact that I had allowed someone to hurt me the way Mark did. I lost complete control in that situation. I gave way more of me than I was ever willing to give anyone else and it felt like it was all in vain. I sat down and told myself I would never give him access to me again. I blocked his *Instagram* and then sent him a text telling him that I was blocking his number too. I always had to cover all of my bases with him, so even though it sounds ridiculous to tell somebody you're blocking them, I didn't want to give him any room to ever say that he tried to fix us and I never responded. I also didn't want to give him even the slightest chance to say I abandoned him again.

After I had blocked him, I was still hurt but I also felt some level of liberation. I felt like I had taken all of my power back and removed any of the power I had given him to hurt me. Oddly, that made me feel better and it gave me just enough confidence to hit my girls so that we could get fine and go out. I think I had gone out maybe three different nights with different groups of friends. Each night was a night of drunk laughs and freedom. I mean, at the end of every night, I would still have to sleep alone and I would still feel whatever I felt after having ended things with Mark, but I knew I needed to move on. Not move on in the sense of finding something new to lay up under right away, just move on from that chapter of my life as a whole. To wake up every day and not think of him, feel him, or miss him.

I kept him blocked for a full month. I still checked in on him from time to time by looking at his *Instagram* from Safari, but we had absolutely no contact with each other. In fact, rumor had it that he and Brittany were officially a couple. I won't tell you who told me, but I heard that she had created a scripted reality show on the *Zeus Network* and they would be some of the main characters.

I got sort of a kick out of this. All that time I spent with him, each time I had questions about his relationship with her and all the fuss he put up about not being able to be in a relationship, it all boiled down to that moment of Mark choosing Brittany. I can't say I wasn't bothered, but I was finally in a good space mentally and emotionally, so I tried not to put too much in to it. I was also frustrated because although I knew Mark needed some consistent income, he was too talented as an athlete to leave that behind for an acting career that would have him looking like a clown.

Naturally, my overly analytical brain really started rolling. All of a sudden Brittany wasn't crazy anymore? Suddenly, he was ready to be in a relationship? That was interesting, to say the least. I kept telling myself to let it go. Regardless of the fact that I disagreed with the choice, I wanted him to win, whatever way he felt necessary.

I let the whole thing go. I made it a point not to put too much thought into it because I have a tendency to obsess over things and it becomes a black hole.

The universe and me have a funny relationship. It's like as soon as I think about something or someone, it comes to life in one way or another. You know how if you think about something or talk about something and two seconds later, it pops up as an ad on your iPhone? That's how my mind and the universe work. Fast forward exactly one week after hearing about Mark's new relationship and new digital show, I was on my way to the office, minding my business and my phone rings, which is rare at that time of morning and guess who it was. Fucking Mark Miller. What were the chances? I let the phone ring for a while before I answered because, honestly, I wasn't sure I was going to answer at all. I pulled up to a red light, held the phone in my hand and really debated not answering. I didn't want to be available to Mark anymore. The problem was, even though he had hurt me, even though I felt like he did me dirty and that he was a liar, he was still my friend somewhere underneath all of that, so I answered.

I was driving well below the speed limit when I answered and made sure my voice sounded just as confused as I really was. "Mark Garnett. Hi?"

Garnett is Mark's middle name. Whenever I was upset with him, annoyed with him, frustrated with him or wanted to punch him in his shit, I called him by his first and middle name. Ironically, at that moment, it wasn't planned, it just came out naturally. I think he was shocked that I answered more than he was shocked that I called him by his first and middle.

Whatever the case, he didn't let it go unnoticed that I used his middle name. "Damn. I haven't even said a word and I'm already Mark Garnett?" He obviously had a smile on his face.

I start pulling over to the side of the road. Hearing the smile in his voice sort of lightened the mood and eased the tension. I couldn't help but think about how crazy it was that we ended the way that we did and then we were able to just say barely anything to each other and fall right back to who we used to be.

I smiled a half smile when I responded, "Sorry, it just came out. You're the last person I ever expected to hear from, how are you?"

He jumped right in. "You know what, I didn't even think you were going to answer but I said, 'I miss my dawg, I gotta at least try'. So thank you for answering. You always been a real one."

I was flattered, I guess. I gave the best response I could find, "I mean, I do what I can. How's life treating you?"

He hesitated before he answered. "Ah. You know, I can't complain. I just booked a show on the *Zeus Network* with Brittany. It's like a scripted reality type show. I am in a space where I'm open to being in a relationship again so her and I are giving it a real shot."

There was my desire to punch him in his shit again. I don't even know what part of his body 'his shit' is, I just know I wanted to light it the fuck up. I mean, we haven't spoken in a month, maybe more and the first thing he tells me is that he's giving the same woman he said he didn't want to be with a chance. Just like a nigga. The shit was almost comical to me. Anyway, I kept my cool, silenced my thoughts, put on a brave face and entertained his bullshit, as usual.

Luckily, he couldn't see my face but my tone was dry as fuck. "That's interesting. I actually heard about the show part, that's definitely a bit different but I imagine all publicity is good publicity, so I'm happy for you. It's crazy that you and Brittany are together, but congrats."

Mark knew he was outta pocket. I might be crazy, but I think he called me just to tell me that they were together and that they were doing this little *Zeus* project together. I mean, it didn't matter. I had already known, but he didn't know that I knew before that moment. Whenever Mark knows I feel a way about something, he naturally has a story behind why he has been doing whatever it is that he's been doing. That conversation was no different.

He tried not to let his energy shift despite having felt mine shift. "Thank you, Ki. The show is definitely different but I think it will give me a platform to expand a few other outlets I'm going to start working on. As far as Brittany goes, I've always been crazy about her. I think I told you before, like, she's a queen. She treats me like a king even when I'm not acting like one. She acts like my mom sometimes and even though it's irritating, I need that. She really loves me unconditionally."

I was so done with that conversation. He was really saying this shit to me as if I didn't remember damn near every conversation we had ever had, verbatim.

I put on yet another brave face to reply. I couldn't help but laugh a little and then I said, "Well, that's good. I'm happy for you. I hope that works out exactly how you want it to. I have a lot to say" I laughed again. "But I'll stall you out. I just got to the office though, so I'll have to talk to you another time."

The truth was that I hadn't even pulled from the side of the road yet, I just couldn't listen to him lie to me anymore. I'm the last person Mark ever needed to lie to. Ever! I know he felt it. I know he knew me well enough to know that I wasn't buying that bullshit. I hope he did.

There wasn't much left for him to say, so he said the only thing he could say, "Alright, shorty. Have a good day at work. I'll holla at you later."

Obviously, you know that I'm overly analytical and I have to thoroughly process everything thrown at me. So, before we move forward, I want to tell you what I thought about all of this. First and foremost, I thought he was full of shit. I knew that Mark had been having a hard time financially, I knew that he was trying to earn his spot back on an NBA team and I knew that there were other business endeavors he was hoping to launch. In the same breath, I also knew that Brittany had some of the resources he needed to help him with all of that.

She was an actress with a little clout and her father happened to have a heavy hand in the NBA world. I would imagine she also provided hot meals and wet pussy. So, to be completely honest with you, I didn't fault him one bit for it. I actually understood on a very serious level. Outside of any of that, I knew that Mark and Brittany were good friends. If you ask me, they were running a play that would benefit both of their lives and he was doing what he needed to do to benefit his. For whatever reason, I think he felt like he needed to tell me what he told me, before things started to blow up so that I would believe whatever was going to be displayed. I wasn't judging, nor have I ever judged him for that either, because who am I to judge how the next woman or any man gets their bag? I just hoped he wasn't selling his soul to do that.

I say that because the internet is a tricky place. People do things out of their character and allow themselves to be exploited to some capacity to gain the clout that they need to get to the next level of their lives. I didn't want that for Mark. Not that it mattered, but I wanted him to focus on his athletic career and building his other brands without having to attach himself to any type of foolery. In my mind, it would be way more challenging to build his own brand and be taken seriously as an athlete if he was attached to the clown shit of a 'scripted reality' show on *Zeus* that I had already heard about. Regardless, it was Brittany. Mark had chosen Brittany, whether it was real or fake, and I always ended up being right about Mr. Miller. I wasn't sure why, but I was hurt. It wasn't like he was my man. To be honest, I couldn't remember if he was ever really my man. It seemed like we had spent more time in turmoil than we did in tranquility.

SIX

PLAYING THE FIELD

A FEW MONTHS had passed since I had spoken to Mark. The show was a huge hit and even though he wasn't getting any recognition for who he was as an athlete, it was definitely bringing in a fan base that he would be able to turn into consumers, if he played his cards right. Oddly, I was happy for him.

One day I was at the grocery store in the Latin American aisle trying to find the sauce I needed to make my Chicken Molè. I swear, I'm somebody's Hispanic chef. There were two men in the aisle. One of them was attractive but not necessarily my type. I like waves and fades with crispy line-ups, but he had dreads. I have nothing against dreads, they just aren't my shot of *Henny*. Regardless, something about his appearance still intrigued me. As I was looking for my Molè sauce, he and his friend were arguing about whatever they were looking for from their list. It was obvious that a woman had sent them there to grab whatever it was.

The friend turns to me and politely says, "Excuse me, miss. I'm sorry to bother you, but my wife sent us here to get some sauce, but we can't find it. Have you ever heard of this?" He holds his phone up to me and shows me a picture of Worcestershire sauce.

I grab the phone to get a closer look at the picture and laughed at them. "Aw, you guys are cute. It's not going to be in this aisle though. Do you guys grill? How do you not know about this stuff?" I laughed a little harder.

The guy, who is still nameless to me, is so tickled that I'm laughing at them but so grateful that I'm willing to help. "You are so damn nice. We asked that little lady that was here for help and she wasn't trying to help at all. And no offense, but pretty girls aren't even usually this friendly."

We start to walk to the correct aisle and I'm giving him his phone back and I reply, "Well, looks have nothing to do with humility and I have time to help, so why not. I also think it's the cutest thing ever to hear that your wife sent you guys on this mission. It makes me happy to see or hear about young black love."

The oddly-attractive dread head finally cuts into the conversation, "Well, I'm Justin and we can be young black love." He puts his hand out for me to shake it.

I laugh hysterically, shake his hand and say, "Justin, a man of few words. I wasn't referring to us being young black love, by the way."

We were finally standing in front of the Worcestershire sauce so I pointed to the row that it was on so that they could choose whichever brand and price they wanted.

Justin continued, "You weren't? I was just so enamored by your beauty. Like, you're just so effortlessly beautiful and you don't even know that you are. You just on some chill shit today. I can tell. But you must got a baby daddy with a bag or something because that's not a regular MCM bag that you have."

I looked down at my purse and laughed. It was a new purse and he was right, it wasn't like the typical monogrammed bags you usually see, but I had definitely purchased it on my own, I mean, let's be real, MCM bags aren't even that expensive.

I had to ruffle Justin's feathers a little bit and use his statement as a teaching moment. "Wait, so a nigga had to have bought me this bag? I can't just be a woman that works hard for everything and bought myself this bag as a thank you to myself? You decided that because I appear to be chillin' today and you think I'm pretty, a man is behind my bag? Justin, I am thoroughly offended." I said sarcastically.

His friend was hyped! He hopped around making noises that men make when they watch rap battles and then he dapped me up like we were really homeboys. He said, "J. Nigga, you just met your match!"

Justin stood stuck between laughing at his goofy friend slash my hype man and being in awe by the fact that I shut down his entire assumption of me in less than thirty seconds.

He pulled himself together and replied, "Damn. So, you're well spoken, you're beautiful, and you got your own bag. Are you crazy? Why are you single?"

Just to rub in the fact that me and his nameless friend had just become best friends, I stood next to him and put my arm on his shoulder before I answered the question. We all laughed at that moment.

I looked at Justin and then the friend and back at Justin before giving my dramatic response, "I'm certainly not crazy. I'm passionate, as fuck. Picky, as fuck. And I protect my energy at all costs."

My hype man stepped to the side, made his rap battle noises again, dapped me up and then dusted my shoulders off for me. I couldn't help but laugh. I was being so incredibly facetious for no real reason other than I was feeling myself. I don't even know why because I was just wearing black leggings, a black T-shirt and some *Adidas*. Justin wasn't prepared for me. I could tell he was used to being the one that talked all the shit and he was used to women melting at his feet. He wasn't super tall, maybe like five-eleven, he had an athletic build, tattoo sleeves on both arms, a cute little nose and one small dimple on his right cheek. I've never been the one to melt at a man's feet though, no matter how sexy they are or how witty they are. I like wit. I just don't get scammed by it. My ability to be visibly unimpressed and still give you attention as if I am, is probably what had him so intrigued. I knew he was going to ask for my number.

"Okay, miss. I didn't get your name, but we are having a barbecue tonight in the Hills. We are celebrating my boys first year of marriage, you should pull up and vibe with us. If it's not too much to ask, can I have ya number? And your name, too, since you so secretive." Justin said.

I smiled at him and mentally took a couple bricks from my internally built wall, so that I could be nice to the kid for a second. "Sorry," I smiled, "My name is Kiana. Where's your phone? I'll put my number in. However, I can't guarantee I'm showing up to the barbecue in the Hills. That sounds like a setup and I don't have that kind of time."

All three of us laughed. I put my number into Justin's phone. We all said our 'nice to meet you' and went our separate ways. I had absolutely no intention of going to the barbecue, but I was going to entertain whatever nonsense Justin had planned on throwing my way.

Justin was the first person I met after my heartbreak and he was the start of me really playing the field. I have never been the 'get over one by getting under another' type of girl, but Justin shooting his shot was good for my ego; whatever my heart knew, was no longer. I was about to build an entire roster.

A few nights passed after I met Justin, we exchanged text messages here and there, but we mostly talked on the phone and *FaceTimed*. *FaceTime* for me is the equivalent of quality time. So, between that and two lunch dates, Justin and I were having a good time.

I was finally in a groove of not thinking about Mark as

often as I used to, but from time to time, I could feel his energy. I hated it. We had a very sick soul tie so, it's like I knew when he was having a hard time in life, regardless of the reasoning; I could feel it. Whenever that would happen, I would just push it to the back of my mind. I wasn't going to get caught up in that toxic web again. I had been growing so much mentally, spiritually and emotionally and from the inside out. I felt beautiful, powerful, strong and liberated. I finally felt whole again.

One night, I went to a restaurant called *Catch* with my best friend, Tati and her friend, Vickie. We had such a good time that we kept the night going and showed up at *Pinz*, a popular bowling spot, for a birthday party. That's where I met Nate. Nate was about six-three, chocolate skin, beautiful teeth and well-dressed. He didn't have waves and he was really boisterous, but something about him intrigued me. Apparently, I was very easily intrigued at that point in time. I could tell from the way he looked at me, something about me intrigued him as well. My girls and I had no intentions of bowling since we were all wearing heels, but we enjoyed the laughs, drinks and vibes. We sat right in the mix while everyone else was drunk bowling.

Nate would make small talk with the group as a whole, but for some reason, as he was talking to the three of us, I couldn't help but think his questions were secretly directed toward me. At one point, he was asking all of us if we had boyfriends, but my answer was the one he was checking for, so I was very clear when I told him I don't do relationships. I know it sounds ridiculous, but by that time, after feeling that pain I felt with Mark and having dealt with so much other betrayal from friends and family in my past, I had decided that I was going to be single for the rest of my life and I meant it from the bottom of my heart. The open, loving and caring Kiana was packed away and no one would have access to her.

By the time everyone was done bowling, they were all campaigning to meet at *The Good Nite*, which was a little underground karaoke spot they closed out every week. Nate asked me if I was going. Well, he asked us if we were going and we all said no. That's when he told me separately that we should all go, so I told him I'd go for an hour max if my girls were down to go. See, I'm the, 'we pulled up together so we pull off together' type of friend. Long boring story short, we all ended up going to *The Good Nite*.

Once we arrived, Tati and I made ourselves comfortable at the bar. We weren't there to do anything other than enjoy the company of everyone around us. Once Nate arrived, he offered to buy myself and Tati a drink. I declined since I was the DD of the night and Tati got a *Hennessy Sidecar*. Nate made his rounds, greeting everyone, cracking jokes with his friends, hopping in on someone else's karaoke song and kept making his way over to make sure Tati and I were good. He was a drunken gentlemen. Vickie was bouncing around the room, greeting all of her friends. She's always living her best life.

Eventually, he pulled a stool up as close as he could get it next to me and sat down. I was facing forward, elbows on the bar with my phone in hand. He sat sideways, with his legs enveloping mine.

Before even looking at him, I smiled and then turned my head and said, "I take it you know nothing about personal space?"

With a fake confused face, he replied, "Oh, am I too close? Sorry, it's loud in here, I wanted to make sure you could hear me."

I laughed out loud and said, "I've heard you just fine the entire night. Now you're concerned?"

We both laughed and somehow got into a conversation about him not being a drinker, even though he was undoubtedly very drunk. That conversation was cut short because his friends had called him up to join them during their karaoke set. When he left my side, a man came up behind me and attempted to make casual conversation with me. I was hesitant to engage in the conversation because his energy felt weird. Now, I worked with both special needs children and adults for nine years, so I'm always very cognizant of the characteristics of people from the special needs community and at first thought maybe he was special needs. As he uncomfortably continued to talk to me, I realized he was just creepy and drunk. Nate had been in my personal space all night and it didn't feel uncomfortable or overbearing, but this guy was both. He stood way too close to me with his beer in hand and just smiled.

Then he finally said, "Americans just marry one

person, right?" With a creepy smile on his face and a blank look in his eye.

Probably visibly bewildered, I turned my head from looking at him and said, "Yes." As I said that, I lightly tapped Tati's leg to make sure she knew things were getting weird on my side.

The man just stood there looking at me. So I very politely said, "Is everything okay? Can you just back up a little, I'm weird about personal space."

I started looking around the room to see if I could spot Nate anywhere because he wasn't on the stage anymore and I was pretty sure I needed male support in that moment. Besides, the man had only taken maybe half a step back and began speaking half English, half some other language, but whatever he was saying to me included the word 'porno'. At the same moment, I locked eyes with Nate and slightly tilted my head toward the man and raised my eyebrows enough to show Nate I was uncomfortable. We had only just met that night, but I was hoping that he was able to pick up on the signs I was giving him. I wasn't sure if he did, but the man had taken his half step back, forward again, so I tapped my best friend once more to make sure she was also aware of her surroundings. When she turned around, I looked down at my lap and whispered what the man had said to me. She was just as alarmed as I was and she began looking around for a man too. All the men in there and not one was available. Next thing I knew, Nate was next to me.

I looked up at him, grabbed his waist and made sure

the man heard me say, "This guy is talking about porno or something."

So Nate looked at the man and assertively said, "Hey bro, you gotta back up. You're too close to my lady."

Bitch, the man didn't move an inch. He just stood there, drunk and slightly sweaty with a weird smile on his face. Nate towered over this man. He was visibly stronger than him and his voice was so deep it demanded respect. He must have been dumb or incredibly drugged out to have not moved back when Nate asked the first time.

So, Nate took his arm from around me, turned his whole body to the man and said, "Yo, you gotta go. I don't even know how you're in here right now." Then, he proceeded to guide the drunken, smiling weirdo out of the karaoke bar.

The event was a private event, so the bar was closed to the public. So, I don't know how he slipped through the cracks, I'm just glad things didn't get too crazy. When Nate came back to the bar, he pulled his stool up next to mine again.

He got really close to my ear and jokingly said, "We go together now since I just saved your life."

We both laughed hysterically. I took his phone from his hand, held it up to him so that he could unlock it and put my number in it. The rest of the night included us moving from the bar, to a couch in the corner and talking to each other over annoying music, bad singing and lots of laughter. When I finally got home that night, he called me to make sure I got home safely but also to try to convince me to meet up with him so that we could get to know each other more. I opted out of that and we did breakfast the next morning.

The next three months for Nate and I escalated fairly quickly. That's how shit always worked out in my love life though. We went from not knowing each other at all, to basically being in a full-blown relationship. Not literally, that's just how things felt and how quickly things always seemed to move for me. I liked Nate. The more I got to know of him, and besides the fact that he was a Leo, he was a great match for me. He was God-fearing, celibate, hard working with a six figure income, handsome, family oriented, and he had the characteristics of both a leader and a provider.

The problem was that I was serious when I said I didn't want to be in a relationship. I was prepared to never fall in love again. Nate and I would fight about that a lot. You see, Nate lived in love. There was no ounce of him that was ever afraid to feel, give or receive the power of love, no matter how many times love had let him down. I admired him for that. I think it is such a brave and selfless way to live, I just didn't know how to mimic that.

Shortly after meeting Nate, I reconnected with an old fling. This old fling ended amicably in the past. I say that because Tye and I really just spent time together. We didn't talk often and we had sex once during that time. It wasn't anything too serious. When we reconnected though, it was different. Different in the sense that this time around, we were spending real time together, going on real dates, learning real things about each other, and having real sleepovers, both at my place and his. The interesting thing was that we didn't have sex right away, that time around.

Not for lack of time or opportunity, but because I told him that I had begun to lose my connection to sex. He knew that in the past, sex had always equated to an emotional connection for me. Somewhere down the line, it started to feel casual and unconnected. It didn't make me feel good to have casual sex. Well, the sex felt good, but I felt empty after. I needed to have sex with meaning. Tye was a Virgo. My Virgo. He wasn't getting sex from me, so I know he was getting it from somewhere else and I was okay with that because I had his mind and that was more powerful than sex could ever be. It's not to say that he didn't try to have sex, especially nights we slept in the same bed, but I genuinely appreciated his ability to respect my temporary lack of passion for sex.

At that point, my roster consisted of Justin, Nate, Tye and Kevin.

Kevin was a pain in my entire ass and I don't even want to get into the details of how he lasted two months in my life, but he did. Two very long, very exhausting, very annoying months. Kevin needed far too much attention and had zero control of his emotions.

There was also KC, who was a super nice guy, had a lot of money, a felony, was on his way back to jail for a probation violation and had a live-in girlfriend. I was okay with everything except the girlfriend part. He told me about her a few months into our situation, so I cut him off immediately. What do I look like dealing with a man that has a girlfriend?

Listen, I don't know how men continuously have multiple women in their lives. My roster was light and I was having a hard time managing time and energy with all of them. Some days, I would be ready to change my number without notice and be done with all of their asses. Some days, I wanted to pick one and settle down with him. And some days, I felt like a playa-playa. Either way, I gave most of my time and energy to Nate. We bumped heads, a lot, but I liked the way he treated me. I liked the way he noticed little things about me. I liked how much he appreciated me. He and I were the closest of all my boo daddies. I shared more intimate things about myself with him and although he wanted more, I was as vulnerable as I was willing to be with him.

One day we were randomly talking about sports and Nate mentioned knowing a few NBA players. I obviously knew a couple, including Mark, so I asked him who he knew so that I could see if Mark's name was on the list. Of course, it was.

We were on *FaceTime* having this conversation, so I propped my phone up after he said Mark's name and very casually said, "Oh, I know Mark Miller too. I know Matt through a friend of mine and I know Dev through someone else. How do you know Mark?"

I was nervous. I was hoping he didn't say they were friends because I would have to tell him that Mark was my old thing.

Completely oblivious to any of my reasoning, he casually responds, "Ah, Mark is my nigga! We used to hang around a few of the same circles and his best friend and I grew up in the same neighborhood, so we all used to just kick it. It's funny because I heard he is dating this girl named Brittany. Me and her sort of entertained the idea of dating in the past. I mean, it wasn't serious but we tossed the idea around and flirted, I guess you could say."

I was paying attention, but I've never been good at hiding my emotion from my face, so my face must have given me away. It be ya own face, and that's so annoying.

Anyway, something clicked for Nate. Like a fucking light bulb just went off and he said, "Wait. Don't tell me you dated Mark. Is that the nigga that got you so cold-hearted?"

Nervous to hear and see his reaction, I answered truthfully, "I mean he isn't the reason I'm cold-hearted, but he played a part in it. Yes, we dealt with each other for a while."

Nate was hard to read in that moment. I couldn't tell if he was entertained or annoyed. But he continued on, "How long ago was this? How long did y'all date? Did you have sex with him?"

Ah! Those were terrible questions to ask me. I mean, they were the right questions to ask, but if you ask me a question, you have to expect a real answer.

With a Chrissy Teigan fake smile and scrambled eyebrow, I started to answer the questions in the order I remembered them in. "It was recent, like five or six months ago recent. We dealt with each other for quite a while and yes, I had sex with him. Like a lot."

There was no longer a question of whether Nate was entertained or annoyed. It was obvious that he was annoyed. "That's crazy. I don't even see you dating that type of nigga. So, that's the type of nigga you like or what? 'Cus, we will never work if it is. I could never marry you knowing that you dated him. I mean, I don't even think I still have his number, but I can definitely get it. But wow."

Okay, at that point, I was pretty offended and for two seconds, I had lost my mind and then snapped back so that I could respond. "First of all, no one was talking about marriage. Second, I don't know what any of your statements are supposed to mean, but you obviously like the same type of bitches if you tried to date his so called girl, which would make you not too far from being the same type of nigga he is, whatever that means. I guess you tried to flex on me. But that's not even your friend if you don't even have that nigga's number. The only reason I told you about him is because you said y'all were friends. I don't run around telling people who I dated 'cus it's not anybody's business. I only told you because I would never let you shake a man's hand and not know I dealt with him in the past. It was about respect and that was it."

Nate felt my wrath. I was probably disrespectful somewhere in there and ironically, the only reason I now paid any attention to how and what I said to men was because of Mark. But there I was, passive-aggressively defending him and protecting myself at the same time. I don't even know why I felt so defensive for myself or for Mark.

Nate looked at me through the phone with a semi-concerned face. He had never seen me so passionate about anything, so it probably threw him off a bit.

He got closer to his phone and his body language showed compassion when he said, "Babe, I wasn't trying to flex on you. I don't think you understood what I was trying to say. I'm not saying I wouldn't marry you because you dated him, I'm saying I'm not mature enough yet to date someone a friend of mine has dated. I understand why you're saying he's not my friend, but I'm one hundred percent sure if I saw him today, we would pick up wherever we left off."

I hate when men do that. They say whatever the fuck they want to say to you and then try to change their tone after you turn up on them so that you look like the crazy one. I didn't entertain that but I certainly had to dead this entire conversation.

I just looked at him for a second, really more like looked through him because I was staring at him, but I couldn't see him. I had a straight face when I said, "Whatev. I'm over it. I'll talk to you another time." My voice was monotone.

He said, "Alright, babe." He sounded defeated and frustrated.

I ended the call.

Everything went back to normal later that night. Nate had called and apologized for his out of pocket statement and I apologized for snapping at him. I absolutely meant what I said, but I know I could have delivered it more tactfully. I'm not above being accountable for my behavior. A few days had gone by since that conversation and Mark had been heavy on my mind since that day. It was fairly upsetting for me because I thought that I had been completely past that entire situation. I thought that I had moved on and was no longer concerned about him, but it was obvious that I wasn't past it if I still felt some type of way when I thought of him. Once I allowed that door to open and those feelings to resurface, I could feel him again. The soul tie I thought I had broken was still very strong and it damn near consumed my soul.

With Mark, everything had always been a mind versus heart battle. The thing is, there should have been no battle at all. We were done. He was in a relationship and I was doing my own thing. The battle in my head was that he was as happy as he had ever been. The battle in my heart said that his relationship was basically a publicity stunt. My head always won those battles, but the universe always won the entire war.

A week after the conversation with Nate and processing my feelings about it, I unblocked his *Instagram*. Low and behold, he liked an older post of mine about a week after that. Go. Fucking. Figure. I probably shouldn't have unblocked him, but I looked at his page silently; I didn't like one picture or view one story. That was his pattern. Whenever we used to have small beef, whenever we would go periods of time without speaking, he would start making his return by liking my picture. I was confused though. He was in this relationship that appeared to be so perfect and he looked like he was so happy, so why was he trying to make his way back into my life?

I remember calling all of my boos back to back that day. I knew they would either take my mind off of him or irritate me, which would also take my mind off of him. Either way, I needed an outlet as quickly as possible. I called Nate last, because I knew he and I would talk the longest. I debated whether or not I should tell him that Mark had liked my picture and ultimately decided that I would because he was always so open and honest with me about the women in his life. We had been on the phone for probably thirty minutes before I decided to bring Mark up.

I was casual in my delivery when I said, "Oh, guess who liked my picture today. So random."

Seemingly unbothered, Nate replied, "Probably Mark. You wouldn't say that if it was anybody else, so how does that make you feel?"

Shocked that he knew who I was referring to and confused whether he was being sarcastic in his response, I answered his question as honestly as possible. "Uhm, surprised honestly. We didn't end well and our last conversation had a weird vibe and he looks happy in his little relationship. I also know him to like my pictures when he's about to make his grand re-entrance into my life, so I'm confused as to why he would be making his way back."

Nate had completely removed how he felt for me from that conversation and really just acted as my friend. "Ki, that relationship is not real. Whatever they're doing for a check, does not include a real, intimate relationship. I was at an event not too long ago and they were both there and she was texting me while he was literally on the other side of the room. The Brittany I know, would never."

Okay, so my first thought, because I'm a child was, *why the hell didn't he tell me he saw them at an event? Men are so stupid. My girls would have sent me a live play-by-play!*

I snapped out of it and replied, "That's deep. Whatever the case, he chose her, so there is no reason for us to have contact with one another. I think we were really great friends, but he did me dirty and that's just that."

Nate seamlessly changed the topic, "Ok, so what are we eating for dinner tonight?"

I was happy he did. We didn't need to continue to give that topic energy. Well, I didn't. Nate rightfully didn't give a damn.

Later that night, I was thinking about how small the world was. Even though I barely met any of Mark's friends during our situation, we did have a number of mutual friends that I spoke to regularly, but what were the chances that he and Nate knew each other? Apparently, there's only like three social groups in L.A. and somehow, we are all connected. How annoying. I had also started thinking about my relationship with Nate. I liked him. For what it's worth, I liked him more than I liked all of the other men in my life. We had talked a few times about taking things more seriously and as much as I liked him, I didn't want to be with Nate.

I think if I was in a space where I wanted to be in a committed relationship, it would have been with him. I just wasn't anywhere close to wanting that for myself. I felt like maybe I was starting to lead him on. In a way, I was actually doing to him what Mark had done to me because I knew I didn't want to be with him. I also really enjoyed the companionship, attention and affection he provided. I didn't want to lose him, but I didn't want to hurt him either.

For the next twenty-four hours, I put an immense amount of thought into our situation. I really took into consideration how I felt about him. How I felt in general and if I was honestly ready to settle down. I know you're probably thinking that settling down sounds so extreme, but Nate wasn't the date for fun type of guy. He was the type of guy that could meet you today and marry you tomorrow. His feelings for me were growing at a rapid pace.

Ultimately, I decided that the best thing to do was end things with him. I knew that I didn't feel the same way he did and I don't have enough savage in me to just allow a person to continuously fall deeper for me when I am certain I have no intentions of catching feelings, no matter how good they may make me feel.

Within a few days, I told Nate that we needed to end things. I was honest in my reasoning and I felt terrible about it, but it felt like the right thing to do. He's such an incredible man, I knew I would be doing him a disservice if I kept entertaining the idea of 'us' knowing that I had no real intentions of being his. Great man, poor timing. I kept all my other boo daddies with no ill feelings because I knew they all had their own shit poppin' outside of me, so they were welcome to stay as long as they didn't catch real feelings. That included Tye, because outside of Nate, he was the only other one I could really see myself being with.

SEVEN

MAGNETIC

ENDING things with Nate wasn't an emotional experience for me. To be honest, outside of Mark and one of my
exes, men don't take me to an emotional place. I don't
give them that power. Essentially, when it comes to men,
I'm dead inside. Mark resuscitated me and left. Nate has
all the cords I needed to be revived again and I refused. I
felt bad because I knew that to some extent, I led him on
and that's rude, but I wasn't hurt. Also, being that Nate
literally lived in love, I was completely confident that he
would bounce back; he was a great catch.

The other men on my roster kept me busy, so my
mind was always occupied. I was talking to a friend of
mine, Stephon, about it and he was telling me how much
of a savage I was for always keeping it real with these

niggas. I didn't think I was a savage though, I just believe in being honest because I expect honesty. Stephon is one of my closest friends. I literally tell him about every single one of my boo daddies and he's my biggest cheerleader. He's a rapper and happens to be really great friends with Mark, as if my world needed to be any smaller. Mark and Stephon grew up together, so they've known each other way longer. They're men, so they obviously have a different relationship than Stephon and I do, but Stephon and I have a brother/sister relationship, which makes us closer. I like sharing stories with him because he always gives me great male perspective and keeps me in check if I ever get too deep into my emotions, which is generally rare, if we eliminate Mark. The other thing is that since he and Mark are such great friends, I used to try not to put him in a position where he had to give me advice for or against his friend.

We talk just about every day, but at the very least, four times a week because he lives in Vegas. We have to make sure we are constantly up to date on each other's lives. He was coming to L.A. for a few days for a few studio sessions he had lined up and as usual, I would have to pull up on him. At the time, I didn't have anything to do with the music industry professionally, but Stephon trusted my opinion in his music and liked to have my energy in the studio while he created. I always made sure to show up to at least one session. The first night he was recording, it was a late night session, so I went bowling with my friends first and then I pulled up to the studio at about midnight.

It was a smaller room, but when I walked in, immediately I realize that this studio belonged to a friend of Brittany's and I laughed to myself because I don't understand how life could really be that small. Anyway, as I enter the room, Stephon begins to introduce me to a few men that I hadn't met before, I don't remember their names. To the right of the room, there were two men sitting on the floor, to the back of the room, there was one man sitting on a three-person couch. I knew him, that was the homie, KO. He was one of Stephon's best friends. KO stood up to hug me, it had been a while since we'd seen each other. To the left of the couch he was on, there were two men on a love seat and another guy sitting at the end of the couch on a separate chair.

After I had spoken to KO, Stephon continued to introduce me to the rest of the room. The man sitting directly next to KO had his head down, he was playing with his phone but the room was fairly dark so I didn't even really take a full look at him.

Stephon pointed at him and said, "You know my nigga, Mark."

My heart dropped into my vagina. He looked up at me and I can tell his heart dropped into his vagina, if he had one, too.

He stood up, I took a step back and he said "Oh shit. What's up, shorty?" He put one arm around me to hug me and I wrapped my arms around his waist to return the hug.

My mind was on a whole other planet at that point. I remember shaking the other two men's hands but I couldn't tell you anything about them. After I shook their hands, I walked over to the couch that KO was sitting on and sat next to him. The two couches were basically forming an L, so I was just one body away from Mark, my body facing the front of the room, his body facing mine. Initially, I tried to distract myself by playing with my phone but my hands were shaky and my palms were sweaty. I don't know if you could look at me and visibly see my hands shaking, but I didn't want to risk it, so I put my phone down and put my hands under my legs until I could get a grip.

Energy. I was the only woman in a room full of niggas and I could only feel Mark's energy. He was floored. I am even going to say that he was nervous. I could feel him look at me more than once but he didn't say anything, so if I caught him looking, I just made it seem as though I was glancing around the room. Maybe five minutes passed and everybody was in the room doing their own thing and the beat they were going to record on was playing in the background. I took my hands from underneath my lap, looked through my phone and then turned my head to the left slightly and looked at him.

He was looking at me too, so I turned my head even further left and looked at KO and said, "KO, my nigga! How are you? I feel like I haven't seen you in so long."

. . .

Mark put his head down to look at his phone. I really did want to know how KO was doing, but I had also gotten caught looking at Mark, so I had to play it off.

KO was leaning back when I had turned to talk to him, so he leaned forward and said, "Man, you know niggas just be chillin'. Ain't shit to it."

Mark stood up and walked out of the room. The door to enter or exit the room was right near me, so I barely lifted my head but I watched him walk in front of me and followed him with only my eyes. When he returned, he had a Styrofoam cup in his hand and walked toward the bottle of *Hennessy* that was sitting on the floor to the right of me.

One of the guys that was sitting on the floor when I walked in was closer to the bottle than I was, so before he leaned over to grab the bottle, Mark said, "Yo, can I pour some of this?"

I laughed to myself because that proved my point. My presence had made him so nervous, he needed to drink to take the edge off. We hadn't seen or spoken to each other in close to a year. He was in a full-blown, public relationship with Brittany Vasquez, who a lot of people considered somewhat of a big deal at that time. He was at a studio that one of her friends owned, and there I was making him nervous. None of that is to say I wasn't nervous, because I was.

I just enjoyed the slight turn of the table. Mark poured himself some *Hennessy* and drank it down fairly quickly before pouring himself some more. He sat down for maybe ten minutes and then paced around the room for a minute or two. He made it seem as though he was just working the room. That tickled me too. I mean, I didn't even know I had that much power, let alone over a nigga that had a girlfriend.

The guys were all talking about guy stuff, so I was just enjoying the vibe while they caught their vibe before getting in the booth. KO had written his verse and fallen asleep. Stephon was sitting on a bench writing his verse and shooting the shit with everybody. I hadn't really been listening to their conversations because they didn't particularly have anything to do with me. So, I would just catch little pieces here and there. I don't remember who, but somebody in the room had said something about age. Mark was the oldest in the room and then it was me and then Stephon. I don't know how old anyone else was, so I could be wrong, it doesn't really matter. Mark chimed in on that conversation from a corner he had aimlessly walked to during one of his nervous pace breaks. He said, "Yo, I definitely gotta couple years on at least three of y'all, ain't that right, Ki?"

I was looking down at my phone when he said that because this was their conversation. It literally had nothing to do with me, the only reason I had tuned in was because I heard his voice. When he got through the question, I locked my phone, slid it in between my legs, looked up at him and smiled before I said, "Yeah, 'cus you're an old man."

Everyone in the room laughed and then he smiled

and said, "Oh, I'm old now?" I saw his little eyebrows raise. I could tell it put him at ease for me to respond with typical Kiana sarcasm.

That 'now' part is what probably made it clear to everybody in the room who wasn't aware that we knew each other before that day. I didn't need to be included in that conversation at all, and even though it had been so long since we had spoken, I knew Mark like the back of my hand. He was breaking the ice and testing the water simultaneously; he wanted to know if I was still angry with him or if we would be able to be cordial.

I sat back in my seat on the couch before I responded, and then I said, "Just kidding." We both smiled and looked at each other for longer than necessary.

After that, I knew for sure that even if he hadn't thought about me for as long as we hadn't talked, on that day, in that studio, he realized he missed me. He walked out of the room again and this time when he came back, he sat on his couch again, but not for long because three minutes later, he was up and moving around. He walked to the corner of the room again and stood there for a bit while the guys were talking about their verses.

I was still half-tuned in and half-tuned out so when I heard verse talk, I added my two cents. I looked up at Stephon and said, "Aye Steph, can you write my verse, so I can get mine off first."

Everyone started laughing pretty hard and Stephon cut the laughter off by saying, "Man, I'm not about to play with you. The only reason I'm not writing you a verse is 'cus I know you'll get in that booth and go off."

Mark jumped in on this one and said to Stephon, "If you wrote her a verse, I'm outta here. 'Cus she so real, I know she will get in there and kill it. And I'm not prepared to take her serious as an artist yet."

Stephon laughed and said, "Facts!"

They were gassing me, so I moved to the edge of my seat, dramatically flipped my hair on both sides and said, "At least y'all know I'm lit."

Mark has always loved my hair. He watched me flip it and smiled and shook his head before blurting out, "Oh, you flipping the flat iron too? I'm outta here!" He fake walked out of the room yet again.

My purse was sitting to the left of me and to the right was a sleeping KO, but when Mark walked from the corner toward the couch for the umpteenth time, I thought he was heading toward my couch instead, so I reached for my purse to move it out of the way. I guess he changed his mind on his way over, because he changed directions and walked out of the room instead. When he came back into the room, my purse was on the back of the couch leaning against the wall and he sat in between KO and me. He sat so close to me, he was damn near sitting on top of me.

· · ·

I looked at him and jokingly said, "Just fuck my personal space, huh?" We both laughed and then I moved over just a tiny bit. I mean, the couch was pretty small. KO was still knocked out on the other end and then Mark was trying to get in where he fit in.

Stephon stood up from the bench he was on and said, "We bout to go outside and smoke and then come back and lay these verses."

Everybody, except for Mark and I stood up to leave the room. Even KO got up and he hadn't budged the entire time. I guess smoke was his alarm.

As everyone walked out, Mark put his arm around my shoulders and brought me in for an awkward sitting side hug. He said, "How you been, Kiana mama? You look good, smell good, all that."

Defensive, sarcastic, Kiana responded. "I mean, I'm just tryna glow up."

Mark laughed. He knows me. "You still talkin' shit, huh?"

I realized how high the wall I had built was and tried to tone it down. "Nah, you don't want no smoke."

Ehh. Wrong answer. It's like he was waiting for me to say that. "No. I definitely want all the smoke." He looked me dead in my face when he said that.

I knew he meant what he said. Whatever smoke we had when things ended, he was fully prepared to talk about it and I wanted no parts of it. Naturally, I tried to change the subject by plugging my phone up to the speakers and playing Eric Bellinger's G.O.A.T. We used to always sing that song when we were on good terms, so I thought I would be able to recreate a happier time and distract him from what he was trying to do. I was right. Well, for a moment. We got through maybe half the song before the guys came back inside and when they did, we turned the music off and I handed the AUX cord to Stephon. Everyone sat where they were sitting before they had gone outside to smoke and Stephon had gone into the booth. I was sitting with my left leg crossed over my right, with my right arm resting on the armrest of the couch, while Mark sat to the left of me. I thought that since everyone had come back into the room, we should change our dynamic.

After all, Mark had a girlfriend. Besides Stephon, none of those guys knew we had dealt with each other in the past. I didn't care what it looked like for him, but I didn't want any of them to have even an inkling that I was some type of groupie. I had already felt like Mark had done a lot by including me in conversations and what not. It almost felt like he was trying to claim his territory, but his territory didn't belong to him anymore. Anyway, I guess my body language wasn't favorable to him because he tickled my side knowing that it would make me stop leaning away from him. I sat up straight.

He got close to me only because the music was loud and whispered in my ear, "I know we got smoke, so let's talk about it."

Honestly, I was shocked that he said that to me.

Shocked because of where we were. Shocked because of how long it's been. Shocked because I didn't know what the point of clearing the air would be.

I turned my head slightly toward him and said, "No smoke. We're good. Just leave it where it's at."

He looked at me, stood up in front of me — in front of everybody — and said, "Let's go."

In my life, I'm alpha. I don't answer to anyone and I handle all of my own business and responsibilities. That being said, I love it when a man can come into my life and take charge without being controlling. So, as much as I didn't want to have that conversation that night, as much as I thought it was an inappropriate time because I was there to support Stephon, the assertiveness Mark displayed in that moment was the type of shit I liked.

I looked up at Mark from where I sat. The room was dark but I could still see his face and he wasn't joking — at all. He stood directly in front of me but his body was at an open angle as if to allow me space to stand up and walk out before him. I rummaged through my purse to find a lollipop I had in there because I knew I'd need something to fidget with when we walked out of that room. He waited patiently, and once I found it, I stood up, looked him in the face and rolled my eyes at him. He didn't care, he lifted his arm in an 'after you' gesture and we walked out of the room.

· · ·

A s we left, one of the guys came out behind Mark and said, "Y'all leavin'?"

Mark turned and yelled back, "Nah, bro. We will be right back."

I was thinking to myself, *yeah, right back. Plus I left my purse in there.*

By this time, it was about two in the morning. As we were walking down the hall, Mark grabbed the back of my neck and then put his hand up the back of my head and massaged my scalp. In that moment, I was reminded of how much I had missed him. I didn't allow that moment to resonate, I immediately gave myself a pep talk to stay strong, stand my ground, and not to let him see me cry under any circumstance. I finally stopped walking at a hallway opening because it was the most secluded portion I could see and because I knew my hair wouldn't withstand standing outside in the cold. In this hallway, the walls on either side of each other were probably three feet apart. I stood against one wall, Mark stood against the other with his left leg bent and foot propped against that wall.

H e wasted no time. He put his hands in the front of his sweatpants and said, "We bout to squash everything. I know you have a lot to say, so I'm gonna let you get yours off first."

I kept my head down, and twisted the stick of the lollipop in my fingers. I looked up at him from the top of my eyes. "I said I didn't want to have this talk, so I don't have anything to say."

He rebutted quickly, "Say what you gotta say so I can shut it down."

I was actually offended by that statement because I could tell that he only wanted to let me feel like I said what I had to say, he wasn't prepared to hear me for real. So, I instantly had an attitude. I'm a brat, I don't care.

I looked at him for a second, laughed sarcastically and said, "Nah, we're not doing this." And then I started to walk away.

Mark is evidentially a giant because it seems like he stopped me in my tracks with half a step. He wrapped his arm around my waist, turned my body around, and somehow, I was right back where I started. I gave him the look of death.

Mark didn't let up. He was gentle when he grabbed me as I walked away, but it was still full-court press. "We're definitely doing this. You always wanna act like a nigga until it's time to be a nigga."

I put my lollipop in my mouth and just looked at him. Finally, I took it out and said, "I never want to act like a nigga. You did me dirty, it hurt my feelings and I'm over it now, so there isn't anything to discuss. When I came in and saw you, I was an adult and I hugged you. If I had an issue, I never would have hugged you. So there is no smoke. The air is clear. Let's just leave it where it's at." I put the lollipop back in my mouth and then interlocked my fingers and placed my hands in front of my body.

Mark was visibly bothered by what I said, because he started to rub the waves on his head. "Kiana, I'm sorry, okay? I'm sorry. You keep telling me I did you dirty and I didn't. My mind changed. That's it. But I never meant to hurt you. Above everything, you were my friend. If anybody ever would have asked me about Kiana, I would tell them 'that's my nigga' 'cus you were. I took two Ls when I lost you. You kept telling me that you were just a spot to get my dick wet and that couldn't be further from the truth. I wish we didn't cross that line because then I would at least still have your friendship. But stop walking around saying that I did you dirty. I did not do you dirty. Period. I would never do you dirty and you know that. If I did you dirty, why did you walk in and hug me? You wouldn't do that."

I didn't want to have that talk. I knew that no matter what I said, Mark wasn't going to see things from my point of view. I wanted to appreciate his apology but it was hard. I stood there with my head leaned back against the wall while I processed what he said and twirled the lollipop around in my mouth. The lollipop was how I redirected my focus so that I wouldn't cry.

I took the lollipop out of my mouth, but I didn't move the rest of my body. I stood still and leaned against the wall. I didn't blink at all when I said, "You're only apologizing to me because you're standing in front me. You wouldn't even feel inclined to do so if I didn't see you here tonight. I'm not asking you for an apology. I said it's fine. We can just leave it where it's at."

Mark looked to his left and took a frustrated deep breath. He hated that I was being so nonchalant. He hated that I was refusing to give him any emotion. That's what he meant by 'acting like a nigga'. But I had to do that with him. I had to build the tallest, thickest wall around myself so that he didn't have access to me, especially after all the time that had passed.

He looked back at me, defeated to some capacity. He rubbed his waves again and said, "I miss you Kiana mama. I miss my friend. You look beautiful tonight. I can't even believe you walked into the studio. Can I have a real hug this time?"

I didn't respond. My face was stale as I continued to twirl the lollipop around in my mouth because I was so anxious. Before I could even think to respond, he took a step forward and snatched the lollipop from my mouth. My lips popped as I attempted to keep all the juice in and savor the blue raspberry flavor before it was out of my grasp. I tried reaching for it, but he caught me off guard and moved a lot quicker than I did, so I just stood there and had a dramatic pout on my face.

He held the lollipop above his head. Looked at me and said, "Stop with the lollipop! You need to find another oral fixation!"

I was still pouting and looking up at the lollipop with one of my arms in the air. I wiggled my fingers like a child and allowed my neck to become weak so that my head went back and said, "It's miiiiineee!" I gave him puppy dog eyes to add extra drama to it.

He lowered his arm but still held it out at a one hundred and eighty degree angle and used his other arm to wave me in. "Come give me a hug and you can have it back." He put his lollipop arm all the way up again and used his other hand as a stop sign before he continued, "But, it needs to be a real Kiana hug, not that weak shit you did when you walked in the studio."

I looked up at him, keeping my puppy dog eyes and pouting. He didn't move from where he stood but he reached out and gently placed his index finger under my chin and touched my bottom lip with his thumb. He had a thing for my bottom lip, I don't know why. I didn't move from where I stood so he took a step forward, lifted my arms and placed them around his neck and wrapped his around my waist. I took a step closer to him, raised myself on my tippy toes and gave in to the hug. We stood there and rocked back and forth, not saying a word, just hugging each other.

I broke the silence when I said, "Can I have my lollipop back now?"

He laughed a soft laugh, released the hug and used the lollipop to play with my bottom lip before he put it back into my mouth for me. "I miss you, shorty." He said as he reached over and placed my hair behind my ear.

I turned my head slightly to the side and smiled. "You only miss me 'cus you saw me."

He was in some sort of trance at this point. He bit his bottom lip and said, "Not true. What are you about to do?"

It was three in the morning. I laughed, showed him the time on my phone and said, "Well, since you made me miss the entire studio session, I'm going to *Crave* to get some food and then I'm taking my ass home."

He grabbed my vagina. Totally random. You would have thought he was single or that I was his girl. Neither of those things were true, but clearly, he didn't care.

I pushed his hand down and casually said, "Keep your hands to yourself."

He moved his hand and placed both his hands back inside the front of his sweatpants. "Can I go home with you?" He asked nonchalantly.

Perplexed and slightly offended, I replied with, "Oh, you thought you were gonna apologize and just come slide in after all this time?" I laughed. "You better get all the way real. You're never going to have me how you had me before. But if you want to go to *Crave* with me, let's go. I'm gonna die of hunger."

He had a mischievous smirk on his face when he said, "I can only go to *Crave* with you if I can go home with you after."

I started to walk back toward the studio to get my purse and as I walked away I was like, "*Crave* and my house have nothing to do with each other. See you at *Crave*."

As we approached the studio, all of the guys were coming out. Stephon had my purse and handed it to me. I looked up at him and said, "You're done already?"

He gave me a side hug and answered, "Yeah, we finished it."

I hugged him back and told him I was sorry. Stephon and I were so close, I knew he would call me the next morning to get the details. I also knew he wasn't tripping that things had happened the way they did. Mark ended up walking me to my car and when he gave me a hug goodbye, he palmed my booty. So I just lifted his arms above my waist for him and went on my way. While I was driving, I decided that as badly as I wanted to go to *Crave*, three in the morning wasn't the best time for me to be getting out of the car for some food. Since Mark had said he wasn't going with me, I decided I'd just go to *Del Taco*. Huge downgrade, but safety first.

I pulled into the drive-thru and opened my *Instagram* while I waited. I had a message from Mark that read, 'after all that, you didn't even go to Crave. I followed you, lol, just one exit though.'

I laughed to myself and wrote back, 'you said you weren't going with me, stalker. So I changed my mind and went to *Del Taco* instead. Also, don't DM me like you don't have my number and like your dick hasn't been down my throat a time or two.'

The next notification I had was a text message from him. 'Whoa. I dropped my phone and he jumped.'

I knew that my statement was risqué being that he had a girlfriend, but I was sort of offended that he DM'd me as opposed to texting me. I mean, who did he think he was? Who did he think I was? I couldn't believe Mark was back in my life. We spent so much time apart, he had completely moved on with his life. I was living my best life. We didn't necessarily end on the best terms but somehow, in about two hours, we reconnected that night as if none of those things were factual. We were fucking magnets to each other. It was like a force neither of us could reckon with.

EIGHT

TABLES TURNED

AT NINE THE MORNING, after running into Mark at
Stephon's studio session, I was on my way to *Burger King*
to get some French toast sticks. First and foremost, I need
you to understand that typically, my food choices are out
of this world. During that phase in my life, when my
emotions were going haywire, I just needed to coat my
stomach with comfort. Okay, moving forward, I was
super deep in thought about having seen Mark the night
before, so I don't even know if my music was playing.
Then my phone rang and broke my train of thought. It
was Stephon and I just knew he was about to go off on me
for coming to the session and basically not even being
there the majority of the time. I deserved it, so I was fully
prepared to hear about myself.

I answered the phone how I always do when Steph
calls me, "Gang Gang!"

It sounded like he had a smile across his face from ear to ear. "My nigga. You got niggas out here shook like that?"

Well that wasn't what I was expecting to hear at all. I wasn't sure we were absolutely on the same page, so I had to clarify before I matched his energy. "What do you mean?" I asked with hesitation and a slight smirk on my face.

It was far too early for him to be this hype, but he was. "What? It's only nine o'clock and two of my niggas just hit my phone about you! First KO called me like 'Yo, my nigga, Mark was on Kiana tough last night. I closed my eyes and that nigga was all over the room, answering questions for her, making sure nobody else in the room could talk to her, shit was crazy".

I cut in before Stephon could continue. "Oh my gosh! Do you understand that I thought I was in there gassing myself? Like I noticed all that and some more shit but I thought I was trippin' because I, for sure, felt like he was trying to claim his territory and I knew he was crazy shook at first. The wild part is that KO was sleeping the entire time so I don't even know how he caught any of this from his dreams!"

We both laughed hysterically for a second and then I continued talking, "Ok, so who was the second person? And can you make sure you don't leave details out. 'Cus you tell stories like a nigga and I be needing you to tell them like my girls!" We laughed again.

Stephon was still laughing as he tried to answer the question, "Man, first off, you know my nigga KO ain't ever really sleep. My nigga basically sleeps with one eye open. He will catch everything, every single time. Anyway, my nigga, Mark called me too, bro! Like, all this before nine in the morning! He was just talking about how he ain't know you were about to pull up and how y'all used to rock real heavy."

I know for a fact that wasn't all Mark had said to Stephon, but you know when men tell stories, they just give the key points and leave out all the good details. But, I was so flattered by all of this. It was hilarious to me but I loved that I was receiving confirmation that I wasn't making up what I was observing or the energy I felt Mark was emitting.

Stephon kept going, "You know that's my bro, but I had to keep it trill. So I told him that you was family, so you're always going to be around. He was just agreeing with me or whatever and I told him you one of the realest and most loyal niggas I know so he can't drag you through the mud under any circumstance. So, he was just on some 'I just miss my friend type shit'. You know I ain't trippin', long as you solid. But I'm proud of my dawg, man, 'cus you really had niggas in that studio shook. Niggas was really scrambling 'cus of you and you held yo shit and didn't fold."

Stephon had finally finished giving me the gist of what both phone calls entailed and gave me a brotherly love type compliment.

So with a huge smile on my face, I said, "Ahhh! He was studio shook! That's so great!" I busted into laughter. The soul-fulfilling, bottom of the gut laughter. "Ok, well first of all, his little 'I just miss my friend' line is funny to me because he for sure tried to go home with me. But anyway, secondly, he already dragged me through the mud. All the stories I told you about that one nigga and all the times I was on *FaceTime* crying and telling you all that bullshit, yeah, that was about your damn friend. I tried to leave you out of it. It's so wild that shit played out how it did last night. I mean, he apologized for hurting my feelings or whatever and we cleared all the smoke, I guess. But it's just funny."

I knew Stephon better than he knew himself, sometimes, so I could hear him processing everything I had just said, even though he hadn't said anything yet. Then he said, "Man, that low-key just got me hot but I'll stay out of it. Long as you know he got a girl and long as you keep your emotions out that shit, I'm *Gucci*. I can't see my dawg out here hurt over a nigga. I don't care if it's my brother or not."

He didn't say much in that sentence, but I knew exactly what he was saying to me. So I reassured him that I was ok. "It's all good, neph. I know most of that shit last night was BS. He just wasn't ready to see me. He wasn't prepared to be 'studio shook." I laughed a little. "So he just said whatever he thought I needed to hear, like niggas do. He gotta whole girlfriend, there isn't a friendship left for him and I. He just doesn't know how to close chapters and leave them there. He has to feel like the air is clear and the door is always open. The issue is that I have a soft spot for him, so for whatever reason, I'm incapable of dogging him like I do the rest of these niggas; so I just let him live. I won't front, I'm always gonna love the guy, but I'll never let him have me again."

Stephon was really listening to what I said. Usually, if he is only half listening, he will randomly say 'that's crazy' or 'on everything' or if he had something to say while I'm talking, he'd cut right in, but this was different for some reason. I think maybe he was processing all of the information as a whole. Once I was done, he said, "You know where I stand. I got a lot to say, but I'mma just respect your wishes and stay out of it. I told bro not to drag you, so we can just leave it at that."

I had to lighten the mood, so I turned up my obnoxious side and said, "Awww, you really love the kid. You really think you somebody's big brother, huh?"

We both laughed and the topic finally changed.

Later that day, Mark texted me. It was small talk and very brief, as if he was just testing the water, as per usual. He simply asked me how I was, I replied and asked him the same. He told me that it was good seeing me and that was that. So I thought.

One week later, he called me. It was about seven in the evening when he called and I was sitting in typical L.A. traffic, having a car concert. I was initially irritated when my phone rang because I was really giving my best vocals but I was shocked when I realized it was him. I honestly didn't expect to hear from him this soon, if at all.

I clicked accept on my car console to answer the call through my Bluetooth. "Hi, Mark Miller. Fancy seeing you here."

He laughed a little. "What's up, shorty? How you?"

"I'm incredible. How's life treating you?" I said with a smile on my face.

It sounded as if he was stretching really good when he replied, "You know I can't complain. I just got off set, the car service is taking me home so I'm gonna eat, take a quick nap and then hit the gym. I miss my Kiana mama. We gotta catch up soon."

Mark is an interesting person. He's very calculated in how he moves, thinks and speaks, but so am I. So, sometimes it's hard for me to take what he's saying for what it is. Sometimes, when he says things to me or has said things to me, it's hard for me to decipher whether or not he's being genuine or laying the foundation for something bigger to come. I guess that falls in line with me not trusting him, both then and now.

Back then, he knew I didn't trust him. I had every reason not to. I missed him too, but I wasn't going to say that out loud. "Well, I'm not sure how we can make that happen seeing as you have a girlfriend, but I hear you." I don't know if my voice reflected how my face looked when I said what I said, but my eyes were squinted, my brows were shifted and my mind was racing far quicker than any of my words could form.

As calm, cool and collected as he always is, Mark replies with, "You always think you know everything. Everything ain't always what it seems and even if it was, that situation would have nothing to do with me hanging out with my friend."

You know why this statement bothered me so much? Because Mark knew me and he knew me very well. He knew I was a read between the lines, think outside the box, ask the right question type of person. He knew that wording things the way he did, without confirming or denying anything one way or another, would get my mind going. I told you, his charm is almost manipulative and so is his intellect. Honestly, I don't think it was ever intentional; I think he just didn't necessarily realize how smart I am. I think it has worked on his other women that don't know him as well as I do and I think the fact that I've never called him out on his bullshit allows him to believe he's gotten away with it. The latter is the bigger issue.

Anyway, I responded to Mark's statement. "Taaaahh!" Was my initial response, because he's funny. Then I said, "Maybe it doesn't matter to you, but I respect relationships, so it matters to me. We definitely won't be hanging out in public and you act like you can't come to the house, so I guess we'll just be phone friends."

It was clear that he only heard one part of what I had just said to him. I could hear the inflection in his voice when he said, "Oh, so I'm still invited to the house? 'Cus, I definitely need a Kiana massage. But I need the whole experience; my Kiana massages always ended a little differently."

I laughed very loud! This nigga was really confused and clearly out of his mind. Still laughing, "Man, if you don't knock it off! You can certainly come to the house, but if you thought the happy ending massage was ever still on the table, you're sadly mistaken. You can come hang out and we both keep our hands to ourselves. So, you let me know when you're ready." By the time I was finished saying all of that, I was far from laughing.

Mark said, "I mean hey, I still have an invite to the crib, I didn't even think I had that much, so I'll take it." He was nonchalant in his statement as if he really was taking what he was given with no complaints or rebuttals.

I giggled a little. As much as he got on my very last nerve, as much as he hurt me, as often as I felt like he shitted on me, Mark was a good guy at heart. Somewhere underneath all of his broken pieces, his confused mind, and his desire to succeed in an industry that requires you to be fake most of the time, I think he really cared about me. So, I let up a little, and I do mean a very little. "Yeah, yeah, yeah. The invite expires, so let me know when you're trying to make good on it so that I can find some time for you in my schedule." I didn't laugh or anything when I said that because I meant it. If I had enough time in between extending the invitation and him utilizing that invite, I would have found a number of ways and reasons as to why it wasn't a good idea.

He either knew me very well or was excited that the opportunity to spend time with me was still available to him because one week later, on a Tuesday afternoon, I got a 'wyd' text from him. That text lead to him coming over to see me. This visit was completely innocent. When he arrived at my place, he walked in the door and hugged me immediately. He closed the door without ever having let me go and once the front door was closed, his embrace was tighter and we paced around the living room as one body. When we got to the couch, he picked me up and held me like a baby before he put me on the couch in the same cradled position. He lifted my legs and turned his body to sit right next to me and crossed my legs over his thighs. My body leaned back against the arm of the couch, his hands rested right on my shins. It was such a natural, comfortable position for us. It felt like home for me; it was both fulfilling and frightening.

We just talked about nothing, laughed, reminisced and told corny jokes for a good forty-five minutes. Honestly, it was like we hadn't missed a beat after all that time. It was like all the turmoil we had experienced never existed. He was my friend and I was his and we just enjoyed enjoying that. This 'hang out and talk' vibe went on for about a month and a half before I decided I needed to make myself less available to him. I felt like he was becoming comfortable with this confidential congregation we had accidentally created. Beyond that, between me and you, I also needed to make sure I didn't allow myself to get sucked back into Mark mayhem. He didn't choose me. He chose Brittany. So, he wasn't going to have his cake and eat it too. He needed to know that I could still slip right through his fingers at any point in time.

Me being me, I always have a roster full of starters on the bench, so there wasn't a lack of things to keep my emotions in check, the issue was more or less that I was starting to spend more time with Mark than I did with any of the other guys on my list, so I just needed to scale back a bit. I needed to start treating him the same way I treated any man I dealt with.

Mark would text me randomly throughout the day

just to ask me what I was doing. Sometimes he wouldn't reply after I responded and sometimes he would make brief conversation. So I started to feel like he was asking just to keep tabs on me. It bothered me for a few reasons —but the main one being that he had a girlfriend, so keeping tabs on me was way out of his realm of entitlement. Gradually, I started taking longer to reply and deliberately remained active on *Instagram* while I wasn't responding. It worked like a fucking charm. It created a distance between us that he didn't like and I'm sure it also made him feel like he was losing whatever piece of me he had left. I mean, I was the Kiana that had never missed a phone call, responded instantly to text messages and damn near shared my location when asked or what I was doing; so this was a bit of a shock for both of us.

On a Thursday night, he called me. "What yo fine ass doin'?" He asked, before I really even had an opportunity to properly answer the phone.

I was feeling myself that day, so my smart ass said, "Staying away from niggas with girlfriends."

Without missing a damn beat, Mark said, "Here we go. How was your day?"

I didn't have any rebuttal to that. Honestly, I was prepared for him to be irritated by it but I didn't plan an entire conversation in my mind like I normally did. So, I wasn't prepared. Go figure. I just had to fall in line with a regular conversation, that was boring. "It was cool. You know I'm always living my best life. What can I do for you, sir?"

Taken aback by my question, Mark sounded offended

when he said, "Nothing. I was just calling to see how my nigga was doing."

In order for me to really turn the tables, I had ignore the fact that I was slightly outta pocket and he was rightfully mildly offended. I completely disregarded the tone in his voice when I responded. "Oh, okay. Let me hit you right back, I need to take this call."

There was no other call. I didn't even give Mark a chance to acknowledge what I had just said, I just hung up the phone. Underneath this fake cold heart of mine, I'm sensitive, emotional, and soft as fuck but I had to stay strong. I was about to play a game and to be completely honest, I didn't know what the end game was, I didn't know what the rules were and I didn't know what I wanted when I beat him at it. I just knew I needed to play.

Later that night, I posted a night view of the city onto my *InstaStory*. It was such a beautiful picture and gave real date night vibes. The gotcha-gotcha is that, I wasn't on a date. Even deeper, that picture was super old but I had never posted it before and I knew Mark's over active mind would travel when he saw it. The glory of social media, right? Anyway, just like I expected, two minutes after I posted the picture, Mark viewed it and then sent me a "wyd" text. I responded pretty much instantly with a text that said, "who's askin'?" That was just me being petty. I mean, obviously, he was the one asking, but game. He gave me an "lol, me" with an eye roll emoji in return. So my reply turned it up a notch and said, "Oh, ok, well I'm in the streets."

There was still no real motive in asking me what I was doing. It really boiled down to pissing on his tree. If I felt like he was asking because he wanted to see me or needed something in particular, I would have just been a normal person and responded as such. So after I sent my text, he asked me what I was in the streets doing and my reply was simple, "Looking for you."

That one sent him over. I imagine he read the text expecting a real answer with real details and real locations and got frustrated that it was the polar opposite. I imagine in the moment he realized I was on some bullshit, he dropped his phone into the lap of his sweatpants, locked the phone and took his hand across the waves on his head in frustration. I was thoroughly satisfied with that thought. So I carried on with my night of nothing. I was actually in the drive-thru at In-N-Out ordering animal fries and a vanilla shake, when I posted the view of the city.

I'm a very petite woman, I mean, proportionately petite and I have somewhat of a shape, but I'm small. However, my appetite is that of a man, so I always eat before I go grocery shopping so that I can stay focused while I'm in there. I like to go to the grocery store when everyone should be sleeping or at work because I only like dealing with people on my terms. Judge me hard, I don't care. I say all that to say that at midnight that same 'try-to-tick-Mark-off' Thursday, he text me again. This time, I didn't expect it and had no idea what I would read when I opened the text. I stopped my cart in the produce section, pulled it over to the side so that I could really give this my undivided attention. His message read, "You got me tight right now, needed you today and you was on some bullshit".

That was the perfect example of how important it is to know who you're dealing with in certain situations. Mark didn't need me that day or in the moment in which he was talking about. What really happened was the he got treated the same way I treat niggas I consider disposable and he didn't like how that felt. I told you he was used to a Kiana that was completely transparent with him, but I set out to make sure she no longer existed.

I replied to his text and said, "So then say that next time. Say you need me. Don't just keep asking me what I'm doing like it matters. I'm not a mind reader, how am I supposed to know you need me, if you aren't clear about it?" He never responded that night and I was one thousand percent okay with that because I felt like that was low-key gaslighting.

Yeah, we had rebuilt somewhat of a friendship, but he had a girlfriend, best friends and homegirls that he could have gone to, not me. He didn't need me. Besides, at that point in time, he was never coming to me because he needed me, he was always just laying the foundation to get inside of me; those are very different. I don't believe for two seconds that he needed me that day, I think he just didn't like being treated like he was regular and tried to find a way to reverse that feeling. But this was my game and even though I hadn't figured out all the rules or how you win, he wasn't going to beat me at it.

A few days later, I was sitting in my office, staring at

my computer and all the work I needed to get done that day. I was in a good head space, I had checked in on all of my boo daddies that morning with quick text messages and my mug was filled with hot black tea that I had sweetened just perfectly. I always knew my day was going to be great when I sweetened my tea perfectly. Next to my work computer was my personal laptop. I hadn't told anyone yet, but I was in the beginning stages of launching my own company. I had learned a lot from my position at the marketing firm, I had developed incredible networks and relationships and I felt like it was time for me to take all of that knowledge and those networks and expand it in a way that would not only help challenge and expand my mind and create my brand, but help me and help my friends expand their careers as well.

LowKi Creative was going to be my baby over the next few months and I knew in my mind that I was going to have to balance my load at the marketing firm, being a present friend, a fake girlfriend to however many men were on my roster and build a team for my creative agency. I thrive in that head space though. The idea of creating something new was scary but I thoroughly enjoyed the challenge it created and the fear I felt behind it. As I sat there and thought about my present and my future, my phone started to ring and it scared the hell out of me. I jumped at the sound of the ring, but I was still in my daze, so I just reached over and silenced the ring without even looking at the phone. When I finally looked over, I saw 'Fictional Character' on the caller id. It was Mark. I change his name in my phone periodically based on how he made me feel and what I thought of him at the time. After his last little 'I needed you' stunt, I couldn't take him seriously.

I finally picked up the phone and answered. "Hi, Mark Miller."

He responded calmly. "What's up shorty, how you?" But his breathing was abnormally heavy.

I could feel that this phone call was specific. Like he didn't call me just to catch up or check in, he had a very specific agenda. Naturally, I said, "I'm great. How can I help you, sir? Also, why are you breathing like you're running a marathon?"

He laughed a little bit. "I'm at the park with my little girl and Britt's son. So while they play, I'm getting a little work out in. But I was calling to see what your schedule looks like this week. I was hoping maybe we could grab something to eat and catch up."

Ok. So let's just discuss the first half of that for a second before we move on. Why was he calling me while he was with her child? Why did he feel the need to even mention that part of it? I mean, I'm the biggest advocate for transparency, but maybe this phone call could have waited until you were alone. Like, I was lightweight offended. I felt like he was trying to rub it in my face that he was playing stepdad to his girlfriend's child. The emotionally unstable part of me thought that if he was playing house somewhere, he didn't need to catch up with me.

The logical, calm, rational me was the one who responded. Thank God I can separate the two. "Oh, okay.

That's cute, dad. Uhm, I'm in the office today and tomorrow and then I'm going to work from home for a few days. What are you trying to catch up on?" I laughed. "I feel like you're gonna tell me I got you pregnant, so I can't handle the suspense."

He laughed. "Ah, man. I just feel like you have the wrong idea about our relationship and how I feel about you. I'm not particularly fond of how you view us. I don't think you believe me when I tell you that I care about you or how much you mean to me. But I love you, you are really my nigga. Like, I love Kiana. I feel like we are a hiding space for one another and I don't feel like it should be that way. I know for a fact that I want you in my life, I just don't know in what capacity I want you there. I know you have your wall up, but I just feel like I can remove at least some of the height of the wall and get you on the same page as me. I know it's gonna take some work and I'm down to put in the work if you're down. I'm not saying you need to make an announcement to all your friends that we know each other. But I do want to talk to you more, spend more time with you and I feel like we can pop out together every once and awhile too."

I was really blown away. I mean, studio shook. I had so many thoughts running through my mind at that moment that it was almost hard to reply. I gathered my thoughts as quickly as I could, the ones I could catch, anyway. "Wow, uhm, I really appreciate this level of honesty, like a lot. I'm just a little confused on how you're not sure in what capacity you want me in your life. I mean, you're going to marry Brittany. I think that's great.

I'm so proud of you for allowing yourself to find, feel and accept love at this capacity. You guys are raising your children together, clearly.

From what you've told me, what you have is beautiful. And it's so brave of you to live in this space after everything you've been through. But with all of that, it only leaves room for me as a friend. With boundaries. I'm not coming to your wedding. Your friends don't know I exist. Brittany can never know I exist. So, as much as I want the same relationship you want for us, whatever that is, I'm just not sure how we can actually accomplish that. There's a certain energy we can't exchange because of your situation. And I mean, despite the fact that we've managed to find a space where we can be friends, we both know there's still something more behind that, that we just try to ignore because we can't live in that space. So if you want to attempt to grow our friendship and just get to a place where we trust each other more than we do now, I'm willing to remove a piece of my wall to try that."

Mark basically agreed with what I said because what else was he going to do? I responded in the way that I did, but I also sort of wanted to cuss him out because how dare he wait until he's in a full blown relationship to decide he wanted to keep me in his life! Although I was happy he was able to communicate that to me the way he did, I think his timing was selfish, for lack of a better term.

NINE

LOVE YOU TOO, MAN

VIRGOS AND CANCERS are alike in the sense that they have tough exteriors. They differ in the sense that a Cancer is typically driven by emotion while a Virgo is driven by the logistics of things. I fall somewhere in between, oddly. I'm just a complex human in general. I struggle from time to time with debilitating anxiety and high-functioning depression, so my hard shell is a tad tougher and my ability to reason rationally comes with the ability to comb through one situation with at least one million thoughts over a sixty-second course of time. So when Mark spilled his heart out about knowing he needed me in his life with uncertainty as to where I fit, my mind went wild. I had to take a day to just really process the conversation as a whole and really decide how I would meet him in the middle. For some reason, I wasn't able to dump my mind enough to pick out one solution. The only thing I knew for sure was that if this friendship was going to work, I was going to have to take my guard down a little in order to allow him back into a space I didn't think I'd ever want to open to him again. So I did; I opened both my mind and my heart to the idea of Mark and Kiana being real friends.

Unfortunately, an entire week went by and I hadn't heard from Mark, at all. He would usually have a snarky remark to my *InstaStory*, or send one of my posts to me in a DM to compliment me, or he would have texted or called me. He hadn't done any of those things. I was super bothered by that because what was the point of him telling me he wanted more out of our friendship if he was just going to disappear? It took me back to a space where I felt like him dealing with me was just a sick game for him. It made me feel like he said and did certain things just to see if he still had the power to do so; like it was for his ego and not from his heart.

With starting my new company, I knew I'd need an office space, but I'd also need to save money wherever I could, so instead of paying rent for an office and an apartment, I had decided to get a bigger apartment that had more amenities, a bigger living space and somewhere that would allow me to hold meetings if I needed to. I had been packing my current apartment up and throwing out things that I had no longer needed. I started with the master bathroom and inside of one of the drawers was a box of magnums that Mark had gotten for us but we hadn't used. It brought me back to some of our better days and then it represented a reason to text him and express my frustration for him having disappeared after that conversation we had. I took a picture of the box of condoms and sent it to him with a message that said, "getting ready to move and found these while I was cleaning. It made me mad at you because you wanna be my friend and then disappear for however long!" I closed that message out with the eye roll emoji.

Honestly, the box of condoms had absolutely nothing to do with me being mad at him but it was just what I used to sugarcoat the real issue at hand. I wasn't sure how he'd respond or if he would at all. About twenty minutes went by before my text notification sounded and I was nervous to open the text. His response was lengthy. "SMH. A box of wasted condoms. I bet you're just gonna throw them away. Don't be mad at me, shorty, the phone works two ways. You said you were down and still didn't hit me. I always gotta hit you first."

Sheesh. He was right. I mean, the phone did work two ways and he always hit me first. The way I saw it, he was the one with a girlfriend, he was the one that had hurt me, so he was the one that needed to reach out first if we were going to talk. Probably not the most logical or fair stipulation, but I felt entitled to that much, so I didn't care. At that point in our situation, I tried not to give or show too much emotion. If I had something to say or felt a way about something, I either swallowed it or wrote it in my notes just to get it off but I made it a point not to send him any more essays. Essays was the old Kiana, he wasn't getting her back. Therefore, I kept my text brief and as to the point as I could. "Well, you told me you knew it'd be work. I opened my heart and mind to the idea of our friendship and you got ghost, but I hear you, I will do my part."

Mark never responded to that text message but somehow a brief phone conversation later that night ended up with him being at my house. He claimed he was in the area, but at the time, I didn't live in a just in the area location. But that's how shit worked with us. It was always one extreme or the other, never just simple black and white. Looking back, I think we are actually the blueprint to a toxic relationship. That's wild. Anyway, when he got to my house, I was in super-chill mode. I was wearing a black tank top, with black spandex shorts and my hair was slicked back into a low bun with a middle part. I was watching *The Mask* starring Jim Carey, one of my favorite actors and working on my website for my new business venture. Half of my apartment was in boxes, a quarter in trash bags and the rest still intact. I had the nerve to have candles burning somewhere in between all that chaos because I still needed to have peace and a vibe.

. . .

W hen he finally arrived at my house, I opened the door for him and he just looked at me from head to toe.

I stood on my tippy toes, grabbed the back of his neck and pulled him in for a hug. "Hi, Mark Miller. How are you?" I wrapped my other arm around his neck and squeezed him tight. His hugs were my weakness. He's a skinny nigga but he's way taller than me and still wider than me, and somehow our bodies still fit like a perfect puzzle when we connect. When he finally embraced me back, he squeezed me just as tight as I did him and then copped a feel of my little booty. I laughed and said, "Keep your hands to yourself."

He laughed too and lifted his hands back up to my lower back. "Sorry, I couldn't help myself." He started to let go of me so that he could properly close the door behind him. Once he closed it, I locked it and we walked to my room. My bed had the comforter and sheet pulled back in a triangle in the spot that I had been sitting in with my laptop keeping my spot warm and the movie paused. I closed my laptop and placed it on the night-stand as he took his shoes off and climbed on to the other side of the bed, without pulling the comforter back.

He laid on his back, propped up on a pillow, arms behind his head with one leg crossed over the other. "What are we watching?" He was so casual and comfort-able about it.

As I climbed into the bed and pulled the blankets over my crisscross applesauce legs, I smiled. Then I said,

"Don't be judgey, it's *The Mask*." I sat up with perfect posture to show him that I stood by my movie choice.

Without moving his body, he turned his head slightly to get a better look at me from the corner of his eyes. With a straight face, he said, "First of all, don't sit up straight like that makes it better. Second of all, I love this movie. Push play."

I smiled at him and pointed the remote at the TV. "Want me to start it over?" I was so giddy that he was going to watch it with me.

"Nah, we good right here." He said as he buried himself deeper into the pillows he was propped up on.

We watched the movie for a good fifteen minutes before he started to get touchy-feely. It was juvenile. His hand was just rubbing on my leg under the blankets. It wasn't something that was unexpected, but he had a girlfriend so it just made it different. I mean, I had no intention of doing anything sexual with him whatsoever, but even the fact that we were laid up in my bed, with candles lit, watching a movie, even if it was just *The Mask*, it felt inappropriate. It felt like we weren't supposed to be doing that, so I had to speak on it.

I didn't pause the movie because I didn't want to make it feel too serious, so I just asked him, "So, have you been able to sort out in what capacity you want me in your life? Because like, I don't see any other capacity outside of a friendship. You have a girlfriend. A very public girlfriend. Y'all are getting money together, raising your children together, everything that I've already said. So there isn't any other capacity in which I can actually exist outside of friendship. I'm definitely not being a sidebitch. That's not my role."

At that point, he took his hand off of my leg and started to give me his undivided attention.

I continued. "I'm a wife. Not a sidebitch. Period. So, I just need to know where your head is at so that I can be in that same space or at least meet you in the middle."

He propped himself up onto his elbow and angled his body toward me a bit more. He looked at me dead in my eyes for a second and then looked down at my lips. I was sort of nervous because I wasn't sure if I had given too much too soon or if I was overthinking the original conversation. I also really needed him to stay focused and the way he looked at my lips suggested that might have been a challenge for him. Then, he used his other arm to reach up and touch my bottom lip. I still don't know what it is about this bottom lip that he loves so much. Whatever the case, I pulled my lip in and bit it lightly with my teeth.

He smirked before he started talking. "You know, I knew your little ass would have a lot more to say. Your mind just never stops. It's crazy. I wish I could tell you to just trust me and leave it at that, but I know that's not even close to being possible right now." He took a long, deep, cleansing breath. "I wish I could tell you everything Ki, 'cus you really my nigga. But I can't. No one knows everything. I'm a firm believer in if you don't want anybody to know, you don't tell anybody. So, as much as I want to tell you, I can't. It's not even that I think you'd tell anybody, I just can't run the risk. I'm running the biggest play I've ever run in my life and if it gets out, I can fuck my bag up."

When I'm anxious, I bite the insides of my cheeks and that's what was happening. I was trying to process, be understanding, and find the correct words to use all at the same time. "So, in the same breath that you're asking me to trust you, you're implying that you don't trust me because you won't tell me whatever it is." I squint my eyes, look up for a second to make it clear that I'm thinking about how crazy that sounds and then I continue. "Does she know that you're running this big mysterious play?"

I n true 'Mark is approaching a hurdle and doesn't know what to say but knows what not to say fashion', he rubbed his hand over his waves. "Of course she knows. But she's the only one that knows, our moms don't even know. And it's not that I don't trust you. If I trust anybody with it, it's you. You been solid since day one. I just can't risk it. There's too much on the line."

I don't know what the conversation did for me. A huge part of me believed him and some other parts of me felt like he was just saying what he thought I needed to hear. The issue was that, I had already had my speculations and theories on what was going on in that relationship; so that conversation in some sick way, solidified the sanity of my theories.

I still needed time to process what he had said to me, but at that moment, I responded to what I had processed immediately. "No offense, but I don't care if your mothers know. I don't care who knows. I'm only concerned about me knowing because you're laid up in bed with me. You flirt with me. You're asking me to trust you. You're telling me that you don't know in what capacity we should exist. But at the same time, it's clear that you don't trust me just as much as I don't trust you. So we either work through that, or we don't, I guess."

He was still facing me at an angle, propped up on his elbow. He used his free arm to grab me and pull me down to him. He hugged me and tickled me simultaneously and said, "I fuck with you, shorty. You know that. We gone figure it out. Stop thinking so much."

I wiggled around in his arms as he tickled me and then when he stopped, our bodies were entangled, his body covering mine. My legs were still slightly crisscross applesauce and the top half of me was pinned down, while my arms were wrapped around his body. I lifted my head and innocently kissed his neck. By innocent, I mean it was just a peck, there was no passion, emotion or intimacy about it. His neck was just near my face, so I gave it a little pop kiss. No big deal. Besides, *The Mask* was still playing in the background, that was hardly intimate, right?

Well, I didn't think so. After I barely kissed his neck, I laughed and struggled to free myself from his barricade. "Get off!" I squirmed around and used my hands to lightly push him up.

He tickled my ribs again, which is my weakness, so my body jolted like an alligator on the attack. He grabbed both my arms and placed them above my head, held them in place and began tickle-scratching me. I don't know why men don't know how to tickle correctly. Most of them bite their nails and still somehow manage to scratch while they tickle — blows my mind. He finally stopped tickling me and I stopped squirming around like an injured animal. He released one of my arms from captivity and guided my hand to his dick. I don't know how we got there or what triggered an erection, but it was basically growing in my hand.

That was my real weakness. As soon as I felt his dick growing inside of my hand, I looked up at him and said, "How'd you get here?"

He let go of my hand, touched my bottom lip with his thumb while his fingers supported my chin and replied, "You always do this to me."

I don't know how I was able to get up so swiftly and smoothly, but I did. I got off of the bed and grabbed at his pants, insinuating that he needed to stand up with me. Without hesitation, he did. The closet next to my bed had a sliding door-mirror and I wanted Mark to watch from every angle he could. I put two fingers into the rim of his sweats and pulled him over to me, right in front of the mirror. Once he was there, I slid my fingers across the rim of his pants and we pulled them down together. He pulled his legs out, while his dick stood erect and waiting. I dropped to my knees and circled the tip of his dick with my tongue a few times before I put the entire thing in my mouth and damn near down my throat.

I had only been sucking him off for maybe forty-five seconds before he moaned out, "Fuck!" After that, it seemed as though his dick grew even more inside of my mouth. I like sucking dick, so his enjoyment turned me on and made me want him even more. Something about the vulnerability that a man embodied and the idea that little ole me could provide such immense pleasure makes me wet. I sucked for about thirty more seconds before he pulled himself out of my mouth.

I looked up at him from my knees and wiped my mouth off with my fingers. "What's wrong?" I asked him.

He rubbed his head, took a step back and looked down at me. "I want that pussy." He shook his head in disbelief.

We both knew we were taking this too far. I was on birth control, but he had a girlfriend, so it seemed inappropriate to not use a condom. Granted, it was inappropriate for him to be having his dick sucked and me to be the one doing it, but there's a way to do everything and that probably wasn't it.

I didn't say anything to him after he told me what he wanted. I just started to suck his dick again, but this time, I kept my eyes locked on his. It was a dangerous game, but I lost all of my common sense when it came to Mark, so I played. Twenty seconds in, he stopped me again but this time he seemed to be fairly flustered. His erection was softening and I was confused because that had never happened before.

"You still got those condoms?" He asked as he paced in place.

I stood up and played with his soft dick in my hand while I answered. "No, I threw them away. A condom was never going to work for you anyway. I'm still on birth control though. And we're here now." I paused and shrugged my shoulders a little. "We might as well finish what we started. My karma is gonna hit hard anyway."

Mark was really flustered. I had never seen him this way. In my mind, I knew it's because he didn't want to cheat on his girlfriend. In my heart, I felt like he didn't trust me. Either way, we should have stopped immediately. To be quite honest, we shouldn't have been in that position in the first place.

Mark looked at me, grabbed me lightly by my neck and guided me closer to the bed. Before he laid me down he said, "Condoms were never gonna work but your karma is going to be fine. I'm about to nut too fast, so it's pointless to have sex." Then he laid me down and pulled me toward the edge of the bed. His erection came back. He inserted himself inside of me and it sent a chill up my spine. I missed him so much but I knew I was dead wrong for everything that was happening.

He gave me two deep strokes before he took a second to refocus his mind. He looked at me with a smirk on his face and shook his head. He gave me two more deep strokes. These were with intent. Purpose or passion, maybe? And then he pulled out.

"No! Why do you keep stopping?" I said with excitement. I didn't want to be teased. I wanted to be fucked.

He looked at me and said, "Because I'm trying not to bust!"

I propped myself up on my elbow, grabbed his dick and lead him right back inside of me. Two more strokes and he pulled out and finished all over my stomach. I guess he wasn't being dramatic. He really did finish fast. Faster than he had ever finished before because that took him all of ninety seconds. I wasn't judging him or anything, I just wanted more. He went right into the bathroom, cleaned himself up and then came out with a warm towel to clean me up too. Protocol.

E xcept this time, while he cleaned me up, he did it with fake aggression. "Why are you so angry?" I asked him playfully.

He shook his head with a smile on his face. "I can't believe I just nutted that fast." He shook his head some more. "I know you're talking shit in your head and it's rude."

I laughed hysterically. "You're nuts. I'm not talking shit in my head. You act like this was our first time having sex. Or like I don't know you for real." I laughed again. "I think you're embarrassed and I think it's cute. I'm not worried about how fast you finished, man. You're over thinking, Virgo. Relax."

He looked at me with a fake mad face and said, "I can never talk to you again. I blew it. You just have no idea! Why would you ever be so wet anyway?"

I stood on top of the bed, walked to the side he was standing on and gave him a hug. "You're being dramatic, knock it off." He hugged me back.

We both put our clothes back on and he gathered his belongings so that he could head out. The credits were rolling on *The Mask*, so I took a mental note that I'd have to watch it again.

There was no special valediction when he left, we hugged, laughed at ourselves, and he said he'd hit me later. I knew it'd be a while later.

The next night, I was skimming through different *InstaStories* on my feed and his happened to be up next. I made it a point not to watch his stories because I never wanted to come across a girlfriend appreciation post, so I intended on closing out of the story I was watching before I had a chance to click into his. Just my luck, instead of swiping out, I swiped right into his story and saw that he was at the strip club. I didn't care about that type of thing, like it didn't create any sort of insecurity or jealous feelings within me. The strippers in his story actually had fucking incredible bodies. So, I sent him a message that said, 'yes real bodies!! They look bomb!' He replied almost immediately with, 'Love you.' I literally just gazed at the message for at least thirty seconds.

I couldn't figure out what context he meant it in or why he said it. There wasn't really a reason to have said it in that moment. Not that anyone needs a reason to say I love you, but in this case, he needed an elaborate reason. I didn't know how to respond or if I was supposed to respond. I sent a message back that said, "LOL...love you too, man." Maybe he was drunk and the statement was misplaced. I don't know. I just know that I wasn't going to put more on it than was actually intended. I'd rather make it light and put less than he put on it.

Maybe two days later, I went to a private event at *Pinz*. I loved bowling, even though I suck at it. It doesn't require real athleticism so I would have gone regardless of the type of event. A friend of mine had invited me and I always had a good time whenever I went out with him. At the event, there were two open bars. One bar was at the beginning of the bowling alley and the second was at the end. Basically, if you were lanes 1-15 or 16-30, you had a bar that was easily accessible. My friend and his group of friends were in lanes 16-17, so that's where I was. I had been there for a good thirty minutes or so when I casually looked down toward the front lanes just to scan the place. Low and behold, I see Mark Miller and it appeared as though he had just gotten done greeting a large group. I couldn't believe it. Well, I could, but I didn't even consider the fact that he may have been there too. He hadn't seen me yet, but he was walking toward my half of the bowling alley so I leaned onto the counter/ball rack so that I could get his attention once he passed my lane. To my surprise, as he got closer, he didn't seem shocked to see me. It was like he was intentionally walking toward me.

With a smile on my face, I yelled out "Gang-Gang!"

There were three little steps that you had to go down in order to get from the walkway to the lane area, so I walked toward the steps, as did he. He smiled and said, "I was just about to text you and say I spy. What you doin' here, shorty? Who you with?"

After hearing him say that, it made since why he wasn't shocked to see me. What still doesn't make sense is how he saw me before I saw him. Anyway, I answered his questions, vaguely. "I'm here to bowl and drink and have fun like everybody else."

His demeanor became territorial, so to speak. "Who. Are. You. With?" He said that with extreme assertion.

I looked him up and down with a smile on my face, because this was a different side of him, but I sort of liked it. "I came here with my friends. What difference does it make?" Before he could answer I added, "You look cute, by the way."

He looked over at the lanes that I was a part of and ignored my answer. Then he looked back at me and said, "We're in public, you know we don't do flirting in public." He bit his bottom lip a little and smirked at me.

I was bothered by that statement, so I made sure he knew. "Oh. You got me fucked up. I wasn't even flirting with you. You better get all the way real." When I said it, it sounded sarcastic, but he knew I meant it.

I started to walk away, but he yelled out, "Aye!"

I rolled my eyes and turned back around with an attitude that you could see all over my face. "Fix your face. How you just walk away while I'm still talking to you? Who is this Kiana? I like the Kiana that be in the house and is happy to see me. This Kiana makes me wanna fuck her up. You acting fake right now 'cus I didn't fuck you how I was supposed to."

I was really irritated at that point. But I still had some playful sass in me because I knew his words and actions were coming from a place of insecurity, so to speak. "No. You just don't like seeing me at the same event you're at." Once I said that, I obnoxiously flipped my hair and did a spin so that he could get a good look at me. "You like the Kiana that's contained in the house 'cus can't nobody else see her. And you're pressed about how you fucked me, I told you I don't care." After that, I rolled my eyes and walked away. I turned back to look at him and he just had a fake shocked look on his face. He turned his lips, raised his brows, shook his head and walked away. I smiled. That should have been the end of our contact with each other for the rest of the night so I went on about my business. I had drinks, I bowled, I laughed, I ate French fries; I thoroughly enjoyed myself. About an hour later, the lights were dimmed and I noticed that Mark was tucked away in the cut near the bar.

The funny thing about this is that the other bar was right near the lanes he was bowling in or hanging out at, whatever he was doing. That means, he didn't need to be at my end of the bowling alley — he was just being a little creep. I told my friend I was going to head to the restroom and then snuck away while Mark was talking with a few guys. While I was in the restroom looking in the mirror making sure I was still cute after a few drinks, some bowling and fake dancing, my phone received a text message from none other than Fictional Character. It read, 'you good?' I didn't respond immediately, so a second message came in. That one read, 'where did you go? Gonna head out, wanted to say bye.'

By that time, I was already walking out of the restroom, so I replied to his message with, "Walking out of the restroom." Ironically, the restroom was toward the front of the bowling alley, where his home lanes were, yet somehow, as I walked back toward the other end of the alley, he was coming from the side my home lanes were and we literally met in the middle. When I saw him, I gave a half smile and a shimmy because I knew he was bothered by the entire interaction we had that night, so I tried to erase it all.

We stood in the middle of the bowling alley, where everyone could see us and hugged. It was a brief hug and then he looked at me and said, "You good? Where yo people at?"

Mark was still hung up on the fact that I never answered his question in regards to who I showed up with, so he thought he was going to get an answer then. I had no desire to ease his mind of whatever he thought or whoever he thought I showed up with. "Why are you so worried about my people? We didn't show up here together so, I'm good." I said with a smirk on my face and a mischievous look in my eye. I was doing a lot, but I didn't care.

Mark knew I was being facetious, so he took a step forward, kept his head high while his eyes roamed the bowling alley, clearly making sure no one was looking directly at us and then whispered through his teeth, "Kiana, don't get fucked up." And then he took a step back like it never happened. He was obviously joking.

I found so much joy in that moment I could hardly contain myself. I grabbed the back of his neck with one arm, took a step closer to him and then stood on my tippy toes so that I could wrap my other arm around him, too. Once I was close enough and tall enough, he naturally wrapped his arms around my waist and we were hugging just long enough for me to say, "You have a girlfriend in the streets. You can't fuck me up even if you wanted to. You can't do anything at all, actually, and it drives you crazy. For the first time ever, I win, you lose. Take that L." I casually release my half of the hug and he looks down at me with a smile but I know deep down inside, he's frustrated and both of us are insane.

Right in that moment, a male friend of his approached him to say hi, so I casually walked away but Mark grabbed my arm as I was leaving as if he wanted me to stay. He doesn't break eye contact with the guy he was speaking to, but I look him in the face, stand there for the two seconds it takes him to stop rubbing his little finger on my arm and then I walk away. Once I get back to my lane, my friend asked me if I was ready to leave and I was. We gathered our things, he said his goodbyes to his friends, and we left.

I saw Mark saying his goodbyes to his friends at his original lane when I was walking toward the exit door, but I didn't bother saying bye to him. We didn't show up together and he didn't invite me to the event so there was no reason he needed to know I was leaving. Besides that, a whole entourage including bodyguards and camera men were taking up most of the walkway, so even if I wanted to properly say goodbye, it would have required too much extra work. By the time I got to my car, I had another text from him. "You good?"

I remember thinking to myself, why does this man keep asking me if I'm good? So I quickly replied, "Yes." Mark doesn't like short answers, so I know that sent him over the top because about thirty minutes later, he called me.

It was sort of funny to me that he was going through all of this just because he saw me out in public, didn't invite me, and couldn't figure out who I was with. I answered the phone with a smile on my face and I rolled my eyes, "Yes, Mark Miller, how can I help you?" I know he could hear the sarcasm in my voice.

He didn't care how I answered the phone, I think he was just glad I did. "Yo, you good? Where are you?"

"I told you I'm good already. Why do you keep asking me if I'm good?" I said that with frustration in my voice because I was actually frustrated at that point. I also ignored the second half of his question so I was thinking that maybe my attitude would deter him from noticing.

I was wrong, obviously. He responded back with a little spice himself. "I don't keep asking you if you're good and if I was, that means I'm double checking. Where are you?"

I paused for a second before I answered the question. Honestly, why did it matter to him where I was, what I was doing or who I was with? I didn't think it was any of his business. He had a girlfriend and it wasn't me, so how I spend my time, share my location, or express whether or not 'I'm good' should be of no concern of his. But he's a man and men are territorial. All of those thoughts became extremely irrelevant when I said, "I'm at home, gosh!"

Mark nonchalantly replied, "Good. Get some rest. I'll hit you tomorrow, shorty."

He did all of that, just to make sure I went home after the bowling alley and not some sort of after-hours turn up. Mark was a funny guy because he was a whole live-in boyfriend, had a whole show that he was gaining so much publicity from, but somehow, he was so concerned about my whereabouts. Truth be told, I was punching the air for having said I was at home. It would have been more exciting if I just hadn't answered the phone at all, or told him it didn't matter where I was.

After I had gotten off the phone with him that night, I began to do a little research. I wanted to see what Brittany had been posting about and if any of the things I saw eluded to some sort of trouble in paradise. I just needed to try to make sense of Mark's behavior that night. There were two things that caught my eye. The first being that she was actually in London working; which made things make a little more sense. Granted, a dog is a dog, on or off the leash, but being that she was gone, I understood why Mark had so much time and put forth so much energy to press me that night.

The second thing I saw was a confessional type interview snippet from their show. It was Brittany's interview but I don't know what the question was that prompted her answer, I just know that it was disrespectful as fuck. Long story short, she basically said that he was an ain't shit nigga and whether that was for entertainment or not, there are some lines you just don't cross when it comes to your relationship. In my opinion, disrespecting your significant other to that capacity for some ratings, followers, viewers, and likes was one of those lines. She had him looking like a clown on the show in general, but this really brought out the whole circus and I hated every bit of it. Mark has his ways, he does some nigga-shit from time to time, but I just don't think that interview was the way to express her personal frustration with him. In my opinion, whether it was real or fake, it shows her lack of respect for her man, the one that is supposed to be the leader of her household, but, what do I know?

TEN

LOVERS AND FRIENDS

I NEVER SAID anything to Mark in regards to how I felt about the whole interview snippet I had seen. Although it was plastered all over *Instagram*, I just didn't feel like it was my place to say anything; not at that point anyway, especially since it was hard to tell what was real and what was entertainment. We had just began laying the foundation of our friendship and he was clearly more comfortable and open than I was. A few nights after I had seen all of that, I get a call from Mark. I didn't hesitate to answer because I didn't have a reason to, I was just finishing up the last bit of packing.

His demeanor was different. His voice was somber and he sounded slightly stressed out. "What's up, shorty? What you doin'?"

Once I felt his energy, I was mildly concerned, so my

response matched that. "I'm chill'n. What's wrong? What are you doing?"

By his breathing, it sounded like maybe he had gone for a run. "Ah, I'm just on a little walk right now. I go on walks to clear my mind and figured I would call my dawg to vent."

That was a new opening conversation for us. I mean, for as long as I had known him, he had never openly said he needed to vent. Hell, I don't think he ever even admitted that he needed or wanted my advice on anything, so I wanted to make sure I handled that situation with care. "Ok, go for it. I'm all ears." I stopped packing and sat down on my bed so that I could give him my undivided attention.

Mark took a sigh of relief. I don't know if he was relieved that I was open to listening or relived to finally get whatever was bothering him off his chest. "You know what I like about you? You can give me unbiased opinions or advice no matter what I throw at you. You always give it to me to the best of your ability and you don't judge me for it. So, I guess this *Zeus* thing has really made Britt and I celebrities or whatever; her more than me. Anyway, with that, a lot of bullshit comes and by bullshit I mean girls."

I interrupt with, "Mmhm." Just so that he knows I am actively listening.

He continues, "I mean, I be on some bullshit sometimes in DMs or whatever, I send little text messages here and there, but I swear I haven't touched any of these bitches. They only person outside of B that I can be connected to is you, and no one even knows about that. But girls keep hitting her, sending her screenshots of this or that and I just feel bad for her because it's like never-ending."

I don't actually know Brittany, so anything I know of her is based purely off of research, hearsay and speculation, which could be accurate or far from it. Regardless, she's a woman, so I knew I could level with her on this but I wanted to be sure I asked the right questions so that I could respond properly. "Sheesh. Ok, so I would imagine she understands that women are going to come out of the woodworks the more popularity the both of you gain, right?"

"Yes. Well, I thought she did. Yeah, she does." Poor guy sounded completely stressed out.

"Ok, and in some capacity or another, you need those women on your bumper because it generates more viewers and fans for the show and eventually you're going to be able to turn them into consumers for whatever endeavors you choose to engage in after the show. The thing is that you're naturally a flirt, and now, more than ever, you need to tighten that shit up. You can't let these bitches feel like they have one up on your girl. You can't let them feel like they have even the slightest chance to come in and shake up your household, but at the same time, you don't have to hard curve 'em. You just have to find some sort of happy medium that keeps the fan base lit and doesn't make your girl feel uncomfortable or like she can't trust you."

I imagined that Mark was shaking his head in agreement. He was quiet for a second and then he said, "Yeah, you're right. I gotta do better. I'll figure it out. Anyway, you in for the night? I might pull up on you."

That threw me off a little. I mean, he's venting about feeling bad that his girl feels a way about other women hitting her DMs about him, and he was still trying to pull up on me. Niggas. I imagine Brittany had just gotten home from London if this issue had risen in their household and resonated enough for him to call me.

Mark is a wild boy sometimes, but I have such a soft spot for him — it makes no sense to me. I moved the phone away from my mouth, put my head back, and placed my hand over my forehead because I knew the next thing that was about to come out of my mouth would contradict every thought that just crossed my mind. "Yeah, I'll be here. Just hit me."

Why was I like this? I have no clue, but we got off the phone after that. My million thoughts started immediately. We were in such a tricky space in my mind because we really were becoming great friends, but somehow, we were sort of lovers too. We hadn't talked about the night we had sex any more after the bowling alley, but the bond felt different — good different, but different and that probably wasn't good.

He didn't end up coming over that night but we talked pretty much every day for the next two weeks or so. Between him shooting for the show, being in the gym to master his original talent of basketball, and me moving and preparing to start my company and still working at the firm, we didn't really have time to see each other. I was content with that because we needed to be platonic friends. Seeing each other had proven to be too dangerous for both of us. Phone friends didn't sound so bad considering neither of us had any self-control when it came to keeping our hands off of each other. I had never been in a situation like this one before. Anytime I met someone that had a girlfriend, prior to this, I was automatically no longer attracted to that person.

It baffled me that my situation with Mark didn't have that same effect on me. It didn't make any sense to me that I could still feel so deeply for this man. I was in over my head trying to build this friendship with him knowing that I had all of these suppressed feelings, knowing that we were crossing lines and expressing both the feelings of fulfillment and the discomfort of crossing said lines. But for some reason, I just kept going. Furthermore, it made no sense that I would deliberately ignore the fact that he was in a whole relationship — a public one that I had to see all over my explore page, at that. I didn't even watch the show. Everything that I knew about it was through *Instagram*.

I was walking into the office on a Tuesday morning, with perfectly-sweetened black tea, my hair was super cooperative that morning, my apartment was finally packed up with my move scheduled for the next day and it was my last week as an employee before I was officially a self-employed business owner; I was feeling pretty incredible. I sat down at my desk, went over a few post-it notes that were left on my desk for me to see and then tossed them. Before I got my laptop out and booted up my work computer, I checked my *Instagram* to see if I had missed anything exciting while I was asleep. I had two DM requests from random men that never stood a chance, a few likes on a couple of old pictures and three messages that contained funny memes from friends that know my childish sense of humor. Next, I went to my explore page and the first thing I saw was a still shot of Mark and Brittany's scripted reality show. My heart dropped. I took a deep breath, leaned all the way back in my chair and dimmed my phone screen before I clicked on the post. It was a sixty-second video showing the moments leading up to Mark proposing to Brittany. My heart was damn near pounding out of my chest. I watched the video twice and then closed the app, locked my phone and put it face down on my desk in front of me. I was still sitting very unladylike in my chair but now my fingers were interlocked and placed on the edge of my desk in front of me while I stared off into space trying to catch at least one of the million thoughts traveling through my mind. I don't know how far in advance the show is shot in comparison to when they air the episodes, but whatever the time frame, Mark and I had been talking almost every day. Why in the entire fuck didn't he tell me this was coming?

I picked up my phone to text him and then I put it back down. I felt like maybe I needed to wait; cool down a bit and also give him a chance to tell me himself. After all, it was definitely on the show, but it didn't necessarily mean it was real. I held off on texting him and focused my energy elsewhere. Honestly, I had a pit in my stomach and I felt like I could throw up everything I had ever eaten. I also had meetings to attend and projects to turn in, so I needed to hold it together.

Even though my boss at the firm was sad to see me go, he was incredibly proud of me for venturing off into entrepreneurship because we had built a pretty great friendship. He set up a meeting for me with a friend of his that he thought would be a good networking opportunity for me and this friend alike. My boss' name was Steve and before the meeting began, he came into my office to give me a quick rundown on who I was about to meet. "Hey, Ki. First off, you look like you just seen a ghost so get your life together, girlfriend." We both laughed and that snapped me out of the shock that I was entangled in. Steve continued, "So, the guy you're meeting with today is Darius . He is super connected from sports to music to entertainment, which is why I think you guys would both benefit from knowing each other. He's really laid back, so take him to lunch, get a feel for each other, and just go from there."

I don't know if my 'I just saw a ghost' face was back or not, but I tried to just keep my composure when Steve was done talking. "Ok, perf. Thank you so much for setting this up. I have about fifteen minutes before he gets here, so I'm going to get a few things together and make some reservations so that we don't have to wait long." I closed my eyes, gave Steve a fake air kiss, and hoped I was concealing all of my thoughts and emotions.

Steve gave me two thumbs up, smiled, did a curtsy and walked out of my office. I was relieved. I closed my eyes, took a deep breath, put my head on my desk and said out loud, "Pull it together, Kiana. Pull it the fuck together." I sat up properly in my chair, took another deep breath, rubbed my edges to make sure they were still in place and used my work computer to make quick reservations at the restaurant below the office. As the universe would have it, I knew Darius. Well, I had never actually met him before because he had been working overseas for the last eight years of his life, but I had heard so much about him, I might as well had known him. Darius was basically Mark's big homie — big brother, really. He had told me so many stories about Darius over the course of our situationship, I basically felt like he was my family too. I couldn't believe the timing of this, yet it was really happening. So much for my perfectly-sweetened black tea theory.

Darius finally arrived at the office, so I met both he and Steve in Steve's office. As I approached Steve's office, I slowly took one last deep breath in and exhaled. I walked into the office with a smile on my face and said, "Hi Darius, I'm Kiana!" while simultaneously putting my hand out for him to shake it.

He gave me a hug instead and smiled. "Nice to finally meet you. Steve speaks so highly of you, I was starting to think you weren't real." The three of us laughed.

I transitioned out of the laughter by saying, "Thanks,

friend!" I smiled and dramatically bat my eyelashes at Steve. Then I looked at Darius and said, "I am definitely real!" I laughed. "And I set up real reservations for us downstairs, so let's go eat!" I had a huge smile on my face, but on the inside, I was literally sick to my stomach and not sure if I would even be able to stomach water at that point. I started walking out of the office and Darius followed.

"Perfect. I thought I would have to grab lunch after we met." He said with excitement.

I laughed, "If every meeting I had could be over food, it would be my best life and I would probably be fat. Food is my favorite." By that time, we arrived at the elevator.

While we were waiting for the elevator to arrive, Darius' phone rang and he said, "Oh, this is my brother, it'll be quick." He answered his phone and said, "Motiv8. What's up, big bro?"

As if my world needed to get any smaller in that moment, I was making it smaller by putting pieces of a puzzle together that I didn't even want to play with. Motiv8 is actually Darius' blood brother. Mark told me about him too. Not much, but enough for me to have understood what was happening in that moment. Anyway, Darius and Motiv8 have a quick conversation about whatever and then Darius said, "Oh yeah, bro, guess what! I went to dinner with Millz last night and he said his girl is pregnant. So hit him later and tell him congrats or whatever."

Millz. Millz is what they call Mark. Mark has a baby on the way.

I briefly interrupted Darius' phone call and said, "I'm going to run to the restroom really quick."

Darius shook his head agreeing and smiled and I literally ran to the restroom. I was dying inside. As soon as I closed the stall door, I lost it, literally. I don't even think I had anything to eat that day, other than drinking my perfectly-sweetened tea. I just couldn't control myself. When I was done pouring my insides into the toilet, I flushed it, stood against the bathroom door, shed a few tears and gave myself a minute to pull it together. Before I exited the stall, I took another deep breath, which was obviously the theme of the day, I wiped my eyes and opened the door. This is gross, but I used sink water to rinse my mouth out, washed my hands, and patted my eyes dry with the paper towel before I dried my hands. I had gum in my purse, so I popped one in my mouth, took one last look at myself in the mirror and basically whispered to my reflection, "Keep it together, bitch." I walked back to the elevator where Darius was waiting for me and we went down the elevator.

We carried out our lunch meeting, which, other than my raging internal emotions, went really well. We discussed the logistics of me helping him put together an event for a major celebrity; it would be the first event under my company's name, so I was really looking forward to getting the ball rolling.

The rest of my day was a blur. I remember turning in the two projects I had completed to Steve and sitting in on a meeting with a junior marketing executive to prepare her to take on a few of my responsibilities. I don't even remember having spoken a word at all in the meeting. To be honest, I don't even remember driving home. I could have ran every red light and stopped at every green one for all I know. Basically, I got home by the grace of God. When I got home and closed my front door, it was as if I had just resurfaced from underwater. The entire day, I literally felt like I was drowning. I stripped myself of my clothes as I walked toward my bedroom and tears rushed down my face. There was no gasping for air and no weeping. Just a lot of tears, fast.

I was completely naked by the time I got to my bedroom, and I left all of my clothing on the floor. I usually start the shower and wait for it to get hot before I get inside, but that day, I turned on the water and got in immediately. The water was cold but I didn't care. I knew that it would only last a few seconds since the dial was basically turned up to the hottest level. I needed to wash the entire day away. All of the emotions, having thrown up, all of it needed to wash away in that shower. I never made a single sound, I just showered while the tears flowed for about thirty minutes. When I was done, I sat on the edge of my bed with my towel wrapped around my body until I air dried. Once my body finally dried, I laid down where I sat and fell asleep in my towel. I must've slept for quite a while, because when I woke up, it was dark outside.

The top of my chest had the imprint of the towel, so I removed it, lotioned my body and put on a sports bra and booty shorts. I wasn't emotional when I woke up, but I was hurt, confused and upset. I learned a lot about Mark from every source except him that day. It didn't make sense to me because we talked damn near every single day. At the very least, I was entitled to a warning about the proposal, whether or not it was real or entertainment. We were friends. We were obviously engaging in something more than that, regardless of how inappropriate those dealings were. As far as the pregnancy went, I didn't feel as entitled to that information, but I was the most torn up about it. I absolutely feel like I should have heard it from him when he was ready to tell me; but hearing it in general was really a punch in the gut.

Later that night, I posted a pregnant emoji in my story with "congrats" written over top of it. When Mark watched that story, I removed him from my friends list and removed myself from his friend list. I was ending whatever was going on between us. I just didn't know how I was going to approach him about it.

The next day was moving day. Thank God, because Lord knows I needed to keep my mind occupied. My body just didn't feel well. Mark called me while the movers were loading up and I didn't answer because I wasn't ready to address any of the new information that had fallen into my lap. Truthfully, I didn't want to have to address it at all. I had a business to launch, an apartment to unpack and decorate. The event for Darius was all about brand activation, so it was important, especially since it would be the first event I was stamping my name on. I didn't have time for emotions.

It seemed like moving took the entire day and I was exhausted. I was going to the office the following day, so I decided to put my bed back together before I went to sleep that night so that at the very least, I could attempt to have a good night's sleep. While I did that, I went over everything I wanted to say to Mark. I basically had the entire conversation with myself, filling in the blanks with what I thought he would say, just so that I would be prepared. Two hours later, I was done putting my bed together, I showered quickly and then I texted Mark a simple "hey." Maybe twenty minutes later, he called me.

He was so excited when I answered the phone, "Kiana, mama! What's up, shorty? How you?"

Him being that happy to hear from me made the whole thing more challenging than I had planned. The entire first five minutes of us being on the phone was us laughing hysterically and joking about absolutely nothing. It was very clear that Mark had zero clue that I knew anything and that my petty post had gone smooth over his head. I had to kill the moment with what I really contacted him about. I needed to get it all off before I started a fresh day. Once our laughter died down, I started my speech. "Ok, so I was calling because well, first of all, there's no beef. I was calling just because."

Mark interrupted me. "Of course, there's no beef. Tuh. Why would there be beef?"

I continued, flustered because during my trial run of that conversation, he didn't interrupt me. "Well, be patient, I'm getting there!"

He laughed, "Oh, my bad. Do ya thang."

I took a deep breath. "Ok, so there's no beef or anything, I just needed to address a few things. I don't watch the show, but I obviously saw your little proposal or whatever and I guess I'm just offended that you wouldn't tell me that it was coming. Like, I think I spoke to you the same day it aired, and you didn't even tell me. Whether it was real or not, I just feel like–"

He interrupted me again. "Wow. You're talking to me about TV, that's crazy! About TV you don't even watch, at that! I don't give a fuck about that shit. You think that's how I'm going to propose to my girl? That shit was all cap."

At that moment, my entire planned conversation had gone out the window. When I practiced this, he didn't disrespect me like he had just done. "First of all, don't do that. Don't say I'm talking to you about TV as if I'm some groupie bitch. When I ask you about TV, you get real fake and elusive and don't answer questions, so obviously you want me to believe what I see. That's wild that you just did that. Anyway, seeing that made me feel a way. I already told you how I feel about this whole thing and how hard my karma is going to hit because of it, but seeing that really put things into perspective for me. So that was one thing. The next thing was hearing that she was pregnant. That really took me over. I didn't expect to hear it from you anytime soon, but it definitely was a different feeling for me. Like, I literally threw up because I felt so many different emotions. So, moving forward, we can still be friends, but I am going to have to deal with you a lot differently."

There wasn't a beat of silence before he replied, "Okay, I don't know what you want me to do with that information, but how the fuck did you find out she was pregnant? I just barely found out. We haven't even told anybody yet. Who told you?"

I hated the attitude he was giving me. 'I don't know what you want me to do with that information.' That's wild! I was blown that those words came out of his mouth. Beyond that, it was obvious that he didn't give two shits about how I felt, all that mattered to him was how I found out about the pregnancy. "It doesn't matter how I found out, so don't do that." As much as neither the proposal or the pregnancy were about me, the emotions attached to them were certainly about me.

He was obviously upset, because he started to raise his voice. "It does matter! I'm not going to hide a whole baby, but if this shit gets out before we want it to, it will fuck off a whole bag! I need to know who told you so that I can have a conversation with that person or put out a cease and desist order if I need to. Who the fuck told you? You swear I wasn't going to tell you myself. I'm so excited about it, so somebody took that moment to tell you away from me. I need to know if the person is in my circle or if it was the thirsty ass nurses, because they will all lose their jobs."

I was in awe at how he was reacting. I had never seen him like this. I tried to remain as calm as I could but I'm petty, so I still took a jab. "You always tell me to just trust you, so I'm going to tell you the same thing, just trust me. It doesn't matter who told me, it wasn't on some weak link shit, I know for a very specific reason. So just trust me when I tell you that your lil bag or whatever is safe and no one is going to find out before they should."

He was livid. "Wow. So you're going to sit there and protect whoever told you over telling me when it's clear that it's bothering me? That's crazy. I guess we aren't as close as I thought we were. I really can't believe this shit."

I was still as cool as a cucumber. "Mark, it has nothing to do with how close we are. How many times have you told me that you can't tell me whatever you can't tell me, but then follow that up with 'it's not because I don't trust you', this is basically the same thing. I'm sorry. I am absolutely not going to tell you who told me but as much as you don't trust me, I need you to just trust me in this moment, and trust that I am telling you the information is safe."

"That's crazy. Alright Ki. I'll hit you later, shorty." Mark sounded defeated. He was upset for sure, but he could have very well been hurt that he felt like my loyalty was to whomever told me that information over him.

"Bye." I had attitude in my tone and hung up the phone immediately. Honestly, I didn't care that he was upset. His reaction to the whole thing could have been a lot more respectful. Especially since he was the guy that taught me respect and the importance of it. I didn't come at him crazy with any of the information I gave him, but somehow, his reaction didn't match the action. Essentially, he was upset that I had found out that his girlfriend was pregnant and we had still had whatever it was that we had.

He felt like he got caught up, but that's not a real excuse. I'm sure he probably felt like my loyalty shifted too. The truth was that my loyalty wasn't to the source of information more than it was to him, obviously. However, his loyalty was always to Brittany. He couldn't tell me certain information because of whatever he thought it would ruin, so I couldn't tell him where I got my information from because I needed to make sure he knew that I was only going to give him as much as he gave me.

When we got off the phone, I laid horizontally across my bed and processed it all. It's interesting because I was always conflicted when it came to Mark. This moment was no different. On one hand, I was happy for him and all of his blessings. On the other hand, I was worried about him because I still wasn't sure I believed that his little relationship was about love. At the same time, I was mad at him for downplaying it. I was also really upset for allowing myself to be so open to him that I gave him the power to hurt me again. I was so emotionally distraught that it made me physically sick to my stomach. I knew I'd be fine eventually, it just felt like this was ripping the Band-Aid off and healing the same wound all over again. I knew Mark and I would probably talk again, but I also knew we'd never be the same, so I deleted his number and went to sleep.

The next day, I didn't even bother getting my tea together for the day. One, everything except my bed was packed away somewhere in my new apartment. Two, my perfectly-sweetened black tea theory was out based on the series of events that had occurred the day before. I didn't have much to do at the office anyway. Steve just wanted me to use my last week to make sure all of the junior executives had enough resources not to drive him crazy without me being there. I would also use that time to make phone calls, send emails, set meetings and scout locations for Darius' event. I also found time to search the internet for furniture to create my new home office vibe and pack up my work office. My day was moving fast; life was moving fast but it was good for me. I needed to keep my mind busy with anything other than Mark and all his blessings that somehow caused me pain. This hurt was different than any hurt I had ever felt because of Mark. Like, my heart hurt, but so did my stomach and I didn't feel like myself in general. I didn't like it.

Halfway through my day, I had basically completed everything I needed for Darius' event. All I needed to do next was go view the location and sit with my teams to bring them up to speed. I felt so good about all of it because it was such a smooth operation all together. My emotions were still all over the place, which is what I think was making me feel unwell. I thought maybe I needed to go #2 or something, because I basically had the bubble guts. When I went to the restroom, there was blood in my underwear. Not a significant amount, but more than should be there seeing as my period wasn't going to start until the end of the month. I hated getting blood in my panties — it seems so childish. I cleaned what I could, walked back to my desk to get a tampon and went back to the restroom.

Once the tampon was in place, I threw the panties in

the trashcan. I couldn't believe all the stress and emotions was causing me to start my period early. Whatever the case, I had to stay focused. I went back to my office and sent Darius an email updating him on everything he needed to know and informed him that if he wanted to view the venue with me, he was more than welcomed. From there, I began to put my belongings in boxes. This was such a bittersweet moment for me, but I was so grateful for it. I didn't take any of my boxes home with me when I left the office, I had enough to unpack at home as it was. I was just going to wait until my last day to take my stuff home.

When I got home that evening, I was going to shower and then start on my kitchen. I went to the restroom. TMI, but I removed the tampon and out came a few blood clots, which was both weird and disgusting. I started the shower and got in as soon as the water was hot. I was secretly pissed that I had to deal with a period in the midst of everything else. It was just an inconvenient time and literally too soon. Whatever. I unpacked my entire kitchen and put at least half of it away.

It was finally time to get in bed. It felt like such a long day, but I had gotten a lot accomplished and I was proud of that. Everything was starting to be new in my life and I loved it. I thought to myself, I should get a new car too. I knew it wouldn't happen right away, obviously, but I opened Safari on my phone and started looking at the BMW X6. That's what I had already had in mind, but in that moment, I was making it a mental goal.

I must have fallen asleep while I was browsing

different packages because I woke up in the middle of the night with crazy cramps and I had bled right through the tampon. I don't typically cramp, I had never bled too soon because my birth control sort of regulated my period and there was more clotting, which was also abnormal for me. I don't play when it comes to things like that, so I put on some sweats and took my ass right to Kaiser. Of course, while I sat in the waiting room, a million thoughts ran through my head. Luckily, I didn't have enough service to go on *Google* and self-diagnose myself, but my brain told me that I probably had some sort of cancerous tumor. The nurse finally called me back and we went over what I had been feeling throughout the day, she had me pee in a cup and then undress and wait for the doctor in one of those gowns.

Dr. K came into my room and introduced himself to me. After the introduction, he jumped right in. "Ok, so my first question is, were you aware that you're pregnant?" He was sympathetic in his tone.

My heart dropped and I got chills over my entire body. My eyes filled with tears and I looked down at my hands that were in my lap. My tears were falling into my hands. I shook my head and without ever looking at the doctor, I replied. "No." I lifted my head to look at him.

He grabbed the stool that was on wheels and sat down on it. I guess so he could be eye level with me. "Okay, that's what I figured. Unfortunately, your body is rejecting the pregnancy. You weren't too far along, so there won't be any other procedures needed to terminate the remainder. Your body will naturally complete the process. The nurse noted in your file that you had been using tampons. I am going to suggest that you refrain from using them and use pads until the process is complete. That way, you can ensure the process goes as smoothly as possible."

I was so in shock, I could literally only nod my head in agreement. I didn't have any words. I couldn't find any. Dr. K kept talking and gave me a few pamphlets and I went home. When I got home, I cried hysterically. Again, another level of pain. I turned on the shower and then dug through my boxes to find the pads I had packed away. I only stood in the hot water, I didn't wash my body or anything. Under normal circumstances, I probably wouldn't have been able to tolerate the temperature of the water. I don't even think I was inside of my own body. I turned the water off, dried my body and put sweats on. I dropped to my knees, fingers interlocked and my face resting on my hands. There I was, in the middle of my room, crying hysterically and praying to God even harder.

I don't even remember what I prayed for; I just needed God to hear my cry and ease my pain. I was broken. To be honest, had my body not rejected that pregnancy, I can't sit here and lie to you and say that there would have been a full pregnancy. I remember thinking I wasn't supposed to be dealing with Mark in the first place. I certainly wasn't about to be pregnant at the same time as his girlfriend or fiancé, whatever she was. We call that hood twins and I wanted no parts of that. Then I thought, *well, what kind of woman would I be if I would have terminated the pregnancy myself?* Gosh, I can't even begin to tell you all of the thoughts I had about this situation. All I knew for sure when I was on that floor praying to God was two things. The first was that I had a lot of healing to do. The second was that I would never tell Mark this happened.

ELEVEN

TAKE THE DEAL

I SLEPT on my floor that night. I guess I had pray-cried myself to sleep and stayed right there where I kneeled the entire night. I woke up exhausted; physically, mentally, emotionally and spiritually. I considered calling into the office and telling them I couldn't make it, but I didn't. I had so much work to do, my days in the office were numbered and the countdown to my first company event wasn't going to stop. I don't wear make-up, I just get lash extensions and I might throw some mascara on my bottom lashes if I'm feeling fancy, but, otherwise, lip gloss is as far as it goes for me. That being said, there was nothing I could do to hide the puffy eyes, dark circles or the clear sign of stress that my face carried. I put on some leggings, an oversized hoodie, a pair of *Air Maxes,* and a fitted cap.

That was all anybody would get of me and I was okay with that. Once I got in the car, I put my seatbelt on, grabbed the steering wheel, took a deep breath and said, "You got this," to myself. My eyes watered because I just couldn't believe my life at this time. So many great things were happening in the midst of chaos and I couldn't understand what I was supposed to take from all of it. Like, what was it teaching me? Why did I need to be stronger than I already was? I needed a girl's night badly.

The thought of telling my best friends everything that had transpired over the last, what felt like century, brought me to tears. I started my car, wiped my tears and drove to the office with no music. I was in traffic, of course, but I just used that time to pray some more and decide which parts of my life I was going to share with my friends. I also used that time to remind myself of all the good things I had going and how important it was for me to push through that dark cloud so that I could still accomplish everything I wanted to accomplish.

Over the next two months, I threw myself into work. I had gotten my apartment and office together. Steve and the girls at work had a really special going away party for me at the office and I had told my entire circle about my life. My immediate circle included Tati, Gianna, Stephon and Keith, and outside of them was Kirsten. They were all super supportive in my healing process and nonjudgmental in me being involved with Mark knowing that he had a girlfriend/fiancé.

In fact, all of them felt the same way I did; Mark was with Brittany because it made the most sense for his finances and his career. I didn't have the clout or resources Brittany had to show Mark that I was capable of helping him get where he needed to be. He chose business over love. We all completely understood that. I mean, it was the lifestyle that we were part of. It didn't mean that we agreed, but we understood, and we didn't judge for it. I knew deep down that it would upset Mark that I had told my friends, but Mark didn't get to choose who I confided in or how I managed to get through the series of events I experienced with or because of him.

Beyond that, it was just as much my secret as it was his and my friends would protect my secret, at all costs. I was in a good space. With all the negative that I had gone through, there was always a positive that offset it, which I'm grateful for because I think getting through it all would have taken longer and been much harder.

Okay, enough of the violin playing.

Let me tell you about my first event! Now, I hadn't had the official launch of my company just yet, I wanted it to be perfect and the perfection required a hefty check. But Darius' event was like a soft launch which was in October. Being that I knew Darius and Mark were damn near family, I knew that the chances of me seeing Mark at this event were very high, unless he was out of town or something. Darius and I had actually started to become closer during the planning phases of the event and our future as business partners was looking pretty promising.

I would, at some point, have to tell him about Mark and get used to the fact that I would probably start to see him more often than I would like.

Anyway, the day of the event was insane. I woke up first thing in the morning to do my hair, get my brows done and get my lashes filled. After that, I did one last walk-thru at the venue and contacted all of my vendors to make sure they had everything they needed and were clear on time and expectations. The event didn't start until nine o'clock for the public and the talent would arrive around eleven o'clock, but I needed anyone who was considered staff to be there at eight o'clock so I could give them the rundown.

Side note: Since I partook in messing with someone else's man, I know that I am not above getting ran up on by the disgruntled girlfriend of a man who was sloppy and allowed her to find something she shouldn't have. I can only pray that it never happens, especially at any event that has to do with my money. I would absolutely deserve the run up; I just wouldn't advise it.

Once nine o'clock rolled around, there was literally a line wrapped around the building of guests waiting to get in. Darius and I were absolutely ecstatic. I more than him because I had worked my ass off to put that event together over the last few months. The whole night, I was super hands-on. If a table needed a bucket of ice and there were no bottle girls around, I was the bottle girl. If a table needed glasses removed and there wasn't a busboy in sight, I was the busboy. I wanted to make sure this night was an experience for everyone involved. I knew that the smooth flow, or lack thereof, would set the tone for events, clients and partnerships to come.

The place was packed! Literally from wall to wall where you have to turn sideways and shuffle in between people to get by. A table of young men who had purchased a few bottles of champagne, wanted their glasses removed from the table, so as I was walking by, one of the men lightly grabbed my arm to ask for help. I grabbed what I could and took a few glasses to the back. As I was headed to the back, there was a woman and a man standing in a space between the bar and the curtains that lead behind the bar, where I was headed. The man had his back to the curtain area, but I knew exactly who it was; it was Mark. My heart dropped and I put my head down and rushed behind the curtain.

I don't know if he had already seen me, but I stayed in back longer than necessary just to gather my thoughts and my nerves. There was an open bottle of *Ciroc* on one of the counters, so I took a shot to the head. I didn't even care how not classy I was being. My plan was to go directly back to the table to finish getting all of the glasses and then hide out in the back for a little longer. I made it back to the table without seeing or running into Mark. While I was at the table, one of the guys was asking me a question, so I was trying to listen to him over the music while I grabbed the champagne glasses and finagled them in between my fingers to hold as many as possible. My left hand was completely at capacity and then someone grabbed my right arm. I looked over and it was Mark.

My heart dropped and my mind went completely blank. I gave him a half smile and he reached his arm out to give me half a hug. After that little church hug, he walked away and I didn't even bother grabbing more glasses before I walked the opposite direction. We didn't even say one word to each other, it was so weird. Like, did we have beef or were we friends? When I got to the back to put the glasses in the sink, I had to catch my breath. It felt like I had just run a marathon. I wasn't sure if his girlfriend was with him but I didn't remember seeing her around when we hugged. In the moment, I assumed he wouldn't have hugged me if she was. I figured he wouldn't have acknowledged me at all. I went into the restroom, looked at myself in the mirror and made sure I was still cute. I knew it wasn't realistic for me to hide out all night, I was running an entire event! I walked out of the bathroom, through the curtains and back into the general area of the event.

As I was exiting, Darius was right at the curtain. "Ah! Just the woman I'm looking for!" He was smiling so big.

I smiled back at him, placed my hair behind my ear and said, "What's up?"

We were facing each other during the initial contact and then he shuffled his way behind me, put both hands onto my shoulders and said, "I can't find any of the bottle girls but I need a couple of bottles for the guys at my table and at my lawyer's table!" He was guiding me to the back of the venue and since the music was so loud, he was basically right up on me so that I could hear what he needed my help with. We had finally reached the table and he very briefly told me which bottles he wanted each table to have. "Get them two bottles of *Hennessy*, just find out how many glasses they need and my lawyer is right there," he pointed, "Just get him a bottle of *Ciroc* and three glasses."

The 'them' he was referring to was Mark and his friends. I was listening to everything Darius was saying to me, but Mark was giving me a stare of death. It was literally like he had seen a ghost and like he wanted to strangle me at the same time. I know he was trying to figure out the connection between me and Darius because for the last four years, he had been telling me about his big bro Darius and there I was having a full blown conversation with him. Keep in mind, he's standing behind me with his hands on my shoulders and Mark had no idea that we were new business partners.

Hell, that was the moment he found out we even knew each other. Once Darius was done talking, two bottle girls walked over, so I told them the orders and I could still feel Mark staring into my soul. Both he and I are chocolate and with the dimmed lights in the venue, it made it hard to see facial expressions, but I smiled at him anyway. I was hoping a little smile would have broken the trance he was in, but it didn't — not even a little bit. After I told the girls what they needed, I roamed around the party as far away from Mark's table as I could.

The entire night, I prepared my mind for him to pull me aside and ask me what the fuck was going on. Mark is the ultimate overthinking analyst, so I was sure he had come up with all of the worst case scenarios about the entire situation. On one hand, I didn't want him to think anything was more than what it was. On the other hand, he wasn't my man, we weren't even actually friends anymore. His girlfriend was at least three months pregnant, so I just felt like, ask your questions or continue to think what you want. Of course, I would have answered any question he had, I just had no intentions of volunteering any information.

The night ended and to my surprise, I didn't see him. I won't lie, it sort of messed with my head not having the opportunity to speak to him about what was happening. I knew him so well and I knew he would probably think that Darius and I were some sort of 'thing', which wasn't the case. I also figured he would have probably put two and two together and realized that Darius told me about the pregnancy, which led me to believe he would also probably wonder how or why we were close enough for that information to be shared. Clearly, we share the overthinking analyst trait. There wasn't anything I could do about any of it. Obviously, everything I had assumed was just that — assumption. For all I knew, he could have given less than a damn about any of it. Well, the way he looked at me said otherwise, but still, you never know.

The event went really well, like better than I expected. We reached capacity pretty much immediately and literally had a line of eager guests wrapped around the building hoping to get in. When I learned that information, I took a mental note to reserve a bigger venue the next time I do a high-profile event like that one. Behind the scenes, things were a bit chaotic. Fortunately, I don't think one guest noticed any mishaps and for that, I am super grateful. I stayed behind after all the guests were gone to be sure the clean-up crew was thorough from top to bottom. This event had my company's name on it, so I was going to make sure not a soul had anything negative to say about how it was run. I touched base with Darius before he left and he was so incredibly thrilled with how smoothly everything went that he wanted to meet as soon as we could about the next event he had in mind. That made me feel so good inside. It was like more validation that I was on the right path.

Monday morning, one day after the event, I was up early drinking my perfectly-sweetened black tea with my laptop in front of me. I was in a Trey Songz mood, so his station was playing on my *Apple Music*. I was in the middle of creating an Excel sheet listing the things that went perfect and the things that needed to be executed more smoothly, when my phone rang. I always think I know whose calling me before I look at the phone, based on what time it is. That morning, I thought it was Gianna calling to find out all the tea from the event.

We had discussed the possibility of Mark being there prior to the event, so it only made sense that she called. As the phone rang, I was sipping my tea and placed it down on the table so that I could type one last thing before I answered. When I finally looked down at my phone, my heart did that thing it always does when I'm caught off guard; it skipped a beat and dropped to my vagina. My caller ID didn't say Gi, it was just a phone number — Mark's phone number. I pointlessly fixed my hair as if he could physically see me, my eyebrows were raised so high they were damn near touching my baby hairs, and my eyes were basically popping out of the sockets. Luckily for me, Mark couldn't see me because ya girl was studio shook.

By the time I answered the phone, I had my shit together. "Well, hello, Mark Garnett. Fancy seeing your number in my phone." I was as cool as a fucking cucumber when I said that, which is crazy because my palms were sweaty.

He was smooth, as per usual. "What's up, shorty? How you been?"

I knew what he was calling for and I felt like I needed to be semi-sensitive to that so I turned off the charm and shenanigans and answered honestly. "Ah. I can't complain. Just trying to live my best life. How are you? I'm sure you're calling with questions, so we can jump right in if you want."

There was silence on the other end of the phone. I started doing this nervous laugh that I do when I know that whatever is happening is just as uncomfortable for anyone else involved as it is for me. It literally sounds like something that would be on *Bevis and Butthead*. Shockingly, Mark started laughing at the same time, which was confusing for me because I didn't actually say anything funny. His laugh was actually just as nervous as mine, which made the entire thing hilarious. I started laughing more and the next thing I knew, we were both cracking up for no reason at all.

In the middle of our laughter, I managed to ask, "What is wrong with you, psycho? Why are you laughing so hard?" Just like that, the mood was less uncomfortable for both of us. I don't know how we always do that and I don't know why it always happens that way but it never fails to work. Between me and you, I like that it happens that way. I feel like it makes it so much easier for us to have the conversation we need to have without having all the animosity.

He replied through his own laughter and said, "I don't know, Ki. I guess I didn't know how much I missed you until we just got on the phone. When I saw you the other night, I was shocked. But then you were like working, I guess, so that was confusing. Like, you already have a good job, so I don't understand why you were working at this event. I mean, not that you can't have more money, it just isn't what you do. It was for sure a good look for you, just different. The thing that threw me for the biggest loop though is that you know my brother and I didn't introduce you to him. So I was standing there trying to figure out like, how do they know each other? How are they this damn close and he barely just got back to the States? None of it made sense to me and you already know I over think, so once I started doing that, I didn't even want to be there anymore. I literally left damn near right after you walked away from the table. I wasn't even going to call today but I couldn't help myself." Obviously, by the time he got done with his speech, we were both done laughing.

Throughout his entire speech, I was pacing around my apartment. He hadn't really asked me any questions. We hadn't really discussed the reason we stopped talking in the first place – his girlfriend being pregnant. I still felt the need to protect myself against him, so I didn't want to volunteer any information.

I know I said that I was going to be semi-sensitive and I feel like I was, but I still needed to address the elephant in the room, even if I was the only one that could see that elephant. "Okay, those are all fair thoughts. Let's start with why you weren't going to call?" I felt like a man at that point. You know how when you send a man an entire paragraph of the things that bother you and they only respond to ONE thing that stood out to them the most? That's basically what I had just done, except I was still going to address the rest of the paragraph.

Mark took his time responding to that question, it seemed as though he was making sure he chose his words correctly. Finally, "Honestly, I feel like I needed to let the air clear first. We had a lot of smoke the last time we spoke, so I just wanted to make sure it was cleared out before I came back. Even if I hadn't seen you, I would have called you when I felt like it was safe, but seeing you expedited that process, I guess."

Sigh. Sometimes, I'm not sure if Mark genuinely doesn't understand certain things because men and women are so different, or if he just acts like he doesn't understand certain things so that he can get away with them easier. I think it's the latter. I giggled a little before my response.

"I mean, nothing has changed. Your girlfriend is still pregnant. You still low-key disrespected me over it as if I asked to find out the information, and I am still fully offended by it." I giggled a little more. Not my uncomfortable giggle though. This giggle is the giggle that acknowledges that I heard what you said to me and lets you know I think you're out of your mind but still respect you enough to reply in a tactful manner. In my mind I was yelling, 'The air can't clear, Mark Miller!! Your girlfriend is pregnant', but I didn't say that out loud, obviously.

"I didn't disrespect you at all, shorty. I was caught by surprise that you had known information that I hadn't even shared yet. Then on top of that, you were protecting whoever your source was and that bothered me too because I thought you and I were closer than that. It made me feel like whatever trust I thought we rebuilt and even the newly built trust, didn't exist." He was pretty defensive in his tone, but I didn't take it offensively.

It's frustrating that he didn't see his behavior as disrespectful for the simple fact that if the roles had been reversed, he would have yelled disrespect from the mountaintops. I wasn't in the mood to force a man to see where I was coming from when he didn't even see where he was coming from. The other thing I had noticed was that he was calling the person my 'source', which, to me, said he still hadn't put two and two together and realized that Darius was my source. "I felt very disrespected, but it's all good. It is what it is at this point. You keep saying that you hadn't shared the information yet, but if I had the info and I didn't get it from you, then you had to have shared it somewhere."

Before I could continue, he cut me off. "Kiana! You are basically the CIA!! You find out everything!! You probably already know what I'm having and I haven't even told anybody yet. I should actually call you Ki-I-A because you literally always know everything. It makes no sense."

I start laughing. "K. First off, Ki-I-A doesn't stand a chance, it's so corny. Second, I didn't even look for this information! It literally fell in my lap! For once, I was minding my business and the information just jumped right into my ear." I started laughing even harder because that statement sounded ridiculous and unbelievable, but it was completely factual.

In that moment, something clicked for Mark; two and two finally equaled four. "Wait. Darius told you about the pregnancy? He was one of three people I told and you don't talk to any of the other people. Well, shit, maybe you do. After the other night, I don't even know who you are anymore. How do you know him? I'm not the one that introduced you. Why would he tell you about the pregnancy?" He was thinking logically at that point, not over thinking, so the pieces were falling right into place. I nodded my head yes as if he could see me. That moment of clarity was the moment that I thought he had at the event, but clearly his thoughts were over-crowded and he hadn't even gotten that far.

I had no reason not to tell Mark the truth at that point. I wasn't keeping it from him maliciously, I just didn't see a reason to show all of my cards, initially. "It's so crazy that I just experienced that 'ah-ha' moment with you, because the night I saw you, you gave me a death stare so I thought you figured it out right then. I know Darius through Steve. My boss, well old boss, Steve. I quit working at the firm because I'm starting my own creative agency. Before I left, Steve introduced me to Darius. Darius didn't directly tell me about the pregnancy, we were literally waiting for the elevator when his brother called him and he told his brother. He referred to you as Millz. I already knew who he was based on all of the conversations we've had about him, so I knew he was talking about you. After he said it, I ran to the restroom because I had to throw up. From there, we went to our lunch meeting and have become friends and business partners since then. That's it."

I could picture his face in my mind. That was a lot of information at once, so I knew his lips were slightly tooted, his eyebrows were raised enough to give his fore-head a few wrinkles, and he rubbed his waves at least twice before he responded. "Wow. Okay. Small world. I am a little offended that you didn't tell me about the creative agency but different issue for a different time. I feel a little bit better about the whole Darius thing, but

I'm still bothered that you met my brother without me introducing him to you."

I cut in before he could finish. "Mark, I don't know any of your friends, really. Anytime I have met them, it was either by accident or through someone else. So, this shouldn't bother you so much." I gave him the respectful giggle again, because clearly he's lost it. "But, I am glad that we were able to have this discussion because I knew your mind traveled far with what you were given to process and that made me feel uneasy."

I could hear the relief in his voice as he transitioned out of that conversation. "Yeah. Yeah. Yeah. So, tell me about this creative agency!"

That put a big smile on my face because it was really something I was proud of. "Ahh, man, it's not time for me to tell you yet, but you'll be the first to know when it is."

"You know what, I am sick and tired of hearing you tell me that you can't tell me something. Who are you? Bring back Kiana!"

I laughed, "Oh, please. That has literally happened twice in the entire four years that I've known you. You tell me you can't tell me something damn near every week, so welcome to this bullshit ass club!"

That must have been a silent 'touché' moment for him, because he didn't argue it at all. "Alright, shorty. I'm glad we talked. I gotta make a few phone calls, but I will hit you later."

I had no objection there. I cheerfully responded, "Likewise, Mr. Miller. Talk to you whenever!" The whenever part was petty. We both knew he wasn't going to call me later.

When we hung up the phone, I called Gianna immediately to update her on everything. If things were going to start getting juicy after that phone call, I didn't want to be so deep in it that it became too much to share with her.

Later that night, at maybe eight o'clock, Mark *FaceTimed* me. I have known this man for four years and I think we've *FaceTimed* maybe two or three times, so this really blew me away. I had just washed my hair in the shower and I still had the towel wrapped around it, so I started not to answer because he had also never seen me like that before. Then I thought, *fuck it, he has a whole pregnant girlfriend, who*

cares what I look like! I propped my phone up on one of the candles in the middle of my dining table, made sure my lighting was decent and answered the *FaceTime* with a slight smile and no words; I just looked at the screen. In true Mark and Kiana fashion, he was on the same vibe, so he was just looking at his screen, smiling at me, not saying a word. As women, we pay attention to details when we are dealing

with a man, so naturally, I noticed that he wasn't in a car, a house or any other place I would recognize him to be at. "Are you at a bar?" I broke the silence. "Why are you *FaceTiming* me if you're out with your friends, weirdo?" I chuckled.

Still without using his words, he flipped his camera. "These are my friends." The camera was showing me three empty glasses and when he flipped the camera back to himself, he showed me the half-full glass that he had in his hand. "This is my friend, too." He smiled a devilish smile.

My first thought was why is he at a bar by himself, four drinks in. But Mark is tricky, he doesn't talk about his issues. He handles everything internally or when it's almost too late, so I knew it wasn't the time to address it. "You need to get new friends, those friends suck. The friends that let you go by yourself aren't too great either." I was very nonchalant in my delivery. I'm not his mother or his girl.

He completely disregarded what I had just said to him. "You don't even love me no more, Ki. That really hurts my heart. Like, I can't believe I lost my Ki." He shook his head in genuine disbelief. He was clearly drunk and I wasn't ready even slightly for whatever would come next.

In an attempt at being sympathetic to his state of mind, I was honest and empathetic. "I'm always going to love you, Mark Miller. I just have to do that from a distance. Things are very different now, we both know that."

He was clearly very drunk and had this little drunk smirk on his face and he just looked at me for a while before he said anything and I just looked back at him, trying to study his face to read his thoughts. "What are you thinking about right now? Your thoughts are usually very loud and I usually know what your looks mean, but you've never looked at me this way before, so what's on your mind?"

. . .

He didn't even hesitate to respond. "You're so beautiful. That dimple on your left cheek is frustrating and I love it. And you. I don't understand why I have to lose my Ki. Have you ever lost a key before? You can't get that shit back. What am I supposed to do?" I wish I could describe his look to you. I don't know where any of this was coming from or why, but wherever it rooted from, he meant it with everything in him and that was really hard for me. He waited until he had a girlfriend. He waited until he got her pregnant to realize how much I meant to him? I knew he was drunk, but fuck.

I had to make light of the situation because there was nothing either of us could do with the feelings we apparently both shared. "Oh, please. You can get another key made anywhere, they even have machines in grocery stores now, you'll be fine. As for me, you're just going to have a version of me that you're not used to having and that's okay too."

He sat up straight for this, so I know he wanted to make sure I took him seriously. "Kiana, you're not listening to me. I love you. I cannot lose you."

There wasn't anything for me to say to that. I felt like none of that mattered anymore. Instead of continuing down that path, I just changed the subject by asking him how his day went. Essentially, Mark was having a baby on me. For the entire duration of us knowing each other, I did nothing but love him the best way I could. I tried to help him whatever ways I could. I was loyal no matter what, and reliable for the most part. So, why he all of a sudden loved me, couldn't lose me and looked at me the way he looked at me tonight, I will never understand. As much as I was flattered, I was also offended and hurt. We talked for about an hour more that night and the conversation ended with us exchanging 'I love you' for the first time in our history. I didn't know what to expect next and I was so confused and mildly uneasy with how that entire moment went. I decided I wouldn't tell anybody until I could process it on my own.

I was in bed looking at the ceiling, shuffling through my thoughts. The way I saw it, when Mark and I met, I was only a flower seed, while Brittany was a flower in full bloom. Mark didn't have the patience to nurture my seed and watch me grow nor did he have the vision of how beautiful and strong my roots would become or how bright my petals would be. As time had it, as God had it, I bloomed into something more magical than he ever knew I was capable of anyway. Because of that, I would have to keep my garden closed to him forever. I had decided that night that no matter what, I wouldn't let him in.

For the next two months, he called me every single day. Literally. It didn't matter if it was the first thing in the morning, middle of the day or super late at night, he found fifteen minutes to an hour each day to call me. I feel like each day we grew closer and made this situation harder for ourselves. I don't know if he really intended on just being my friend, but throughout the duration of that two months, we would talk about our past mishaps and things that bothered the other person, and times that we really enjoyed. That felt like a bit more than a friendship, but still in a safe zone because we hadn't seen each other or done anything that really crossed hard lines. If you believe in emotional cheating, which I do, he was definitely doing that. If Brittany had ever overheard any of our intellectual conversations or flirting conversations, she would have flipped their house upside down.

One afternoon, he was headed to the mall near my house, so he called to test the waters and see if I would invite him over. I did, of course. In a weird way, I was nervous to see him because we had been on the phone every single day for the last two months and the energy was through the roof. Seeing him would either make it that much more explosive, or kill it all together. When he got to the door, I took a deep breath in my nose and released it out of my mouth in an attempt to calm my nerves.

Then, I opened the door with a big smile on my face and did a little pose welcoming him into the house. It was extra, but not surprising by any definition of the word. He was clearly really happy to see me, because as soon as I hit my pose, he came at me for a hug that lifted me off the ground. He closed the door behind him while he still had my body lifted off the ground with one arm and then walked into the living room. By that time, I had wrapped my legs around his body and our hug became more affectionate and embracing while he spun us around in a circle. He knew I hated when he did that because it would make me so dizzy. It started off as a friendly visit.

There was no touchy-feely moments. He kept his hands to himself and we just enjoyed each other's company.

He basically just followed me around my apartment as I found things to clean in order to secretly offset my nerves. I had fake cleaned the kitchen, the living room and the guest bathroom. We then made our way to my bedroom so that I could fake clean that too. Somehow, Mark became a product of his environment because as soon as he crossed the threshold from the living room into my bedroom, he was an entirely different person. I mean, night and day! He couldn't stop touching my little booty and telling me that it was getting bigger.

Which was just him gassing me because this little booty doesn't grow. At first, I was staying strong, standing my ground and trying to keep my distance by moving around the room to clean this or that. Mark, on the other hand, completely loss control, stopped me from fluffing the pillows on my bed for what was probably the fifth time and picked me up. He just held me and swayed back and forth. I was constantly trying to figure out his motives, so I just put my head on his shoulder and went with the swaying. I don't know how long it lasted, but when he put me down, he grabbed my hand and put it on his dick – his hard dick.

He had the nerve to look at me and say, "You always do this."

Shocked, I said, "Wait. I was cleaning. You picked me up!" The issue is that I was saying that as I caressed his dick.

He didn't reply. He just stood there while I massaged

him and he played with my bottom lip. I was looking him dead in his eyes while telling myself to knock it off, but it was almost as if I couldn't control myself. He smelled good, looked good, and having his body next to mine felt good. But, this situation was no good, at all. It didn't matter because without breaking eye contact, I pulled his pants down and dropped to my knees. I started sucking his dick with no hands, getting it wet so that I could suck the soul right out of him. I can tell you right now that in that moment, neither of us were thinking about his pregnant girlfriend.

As I continued to suck, he gripped my hair, whispered 'fuck' and then got even harder inside of my mouth. A few seconds later, he gripped my hair into a ponytail and then started fucking my mouth. I closed my eyes and focused on keeping my mouth open and not gagging while he pounded the back of my throat. Before I knew it, he was holding my head in place while his semen swam down my throat. Once he was done, I looked up at him from where I kneeled and shook my head in disbelief with a smirk on my face. He smiled down at me and said, "Still a fucking legend." I got up and went to the restroom to freshen up and he followed closely behind. He cleaned himself with some body wash I had.

We didn't do much talking during clean up, but it wasn't awkward; if anything, it was awkwardly comfortable. There isn't even much more of a story to that moment. We hung out for maybe twenty more minutes and then he left to go to the mall. The next day when he called me, one of the first things out of his mouth was,

"That was a nice little surprise you pulled off yesterday. I wasn't expecting that at all."

"That wasn't a surprise, I think you planned it and I feel bamboozled." I laughed hysterically. "No, but seriously, we have to chill. You have a girlfriend and a baby on the way, this is wild."

As nonchalant as one could be, he said, "Yeah, but I had a baby before you met me too. What does one on the way have to do with anything?"

He has to be kidding. I mean, there is absolutely no way he meant that, but I wasn't willing to find out so I just said, "Anyway! How was your day? What did you do today?" Just like that, I changed the whole conversation. I have always been good at changing conversations if they don't fit the vibe I want. For the next three weeks, I saw him consecutively once a week before or after his 'mall' visit. None of those times included anything sexual, besides him hugging me a lot. It was just us spending time together talking, laughing and watching parts of crime shows because that was always what I had on TV.

On New Year's Eve, he came over before his mall visit, as per usual, but this visit was different. When he got to the house, we hugged like we always did, but when he came in and took his shoes off. He sat at the table, so I followed his lead. His energy was different, off really, so I asked him about it. "What's your deal? Your energy is off. What's on your mind?"

He sat there for a moment. I guess maybe thinking about his answer. "Hmm. You know, I don't really know. I feel different but not necessarily in a bad way, just in a different space right now. I feel like life is moving in a different direction than I wanted it to career wise, so I'm just trying to maneuver around that and I don't know, it's just different." He chuckled uncomfortably when he was done. He hadn't really opened up to me like that before and I could feel that he was leaving out more than he was actually allowing me to know, but I had to just take what I was given. I wanted to make sure I chose my words carefully as to not make it feel like an unsafe place for him to share. I don't know why, but I felt like he didn't know how to share, more than I felt like he didn't want to share.

I gave him a minute before I responded because I wanted to make sure he had said everything he was willing to say. "I mean, your life right now is more different than it has ever been. It used to just be you and the baby that you were responsible for, and now you are not only responsible for her, but for Brittany, her son and your unborn child too. Like, you're going to be a father of three soon and that alone is a huge change for anybody. Maybe you're just in a stage of transition right now in order to prepare you for the next stage of your life. You know?"

He nodded his head to agree with what I had just said. "Yeah, that's true. We did a 3-D ultrasound the other day and it just really put me in a different space. It's so crazy, she looks just like Brittany. I mean, obviously, she doesn't look like what she will look like yet, but I can see Brittany for sure. You wanna see?" He grabbed his phone from his pocket and started to unlock it.

That was where this whole thing got really tricky for me. Mark and I had gotten so close over the last three months that I could honestly say we were great friends. On the other hand, there was that line that we had already crossed and the feelings that I kept as concealed as I could. As his friend, I was supposed to be ecstatic to see these ultrasounds, as the woman he has cheated on his girlfriend with, I wanted no parts. By that time, it didn't matter, his phone was already out and he was about to push play on a video, so I just tuned in. I watched a video of her hand putting maybe four different ultrasound pictures into the camera and I melted inside. He was genuinely so happy about this baby and I wanted to feel that same joy with him. I swear I did, but it was hard. Really, really, really hard.

By now, you know what I do when I am uncomfortable with a conversation, I change it and this moment was no different. As I was looking at the video, I noticed Brittany's nails were orange, the same orange I had almost gotten that day. "Dang, I am so glad I didn't get orange nails today. I literally almost got that exact orange. That's crazy." The video had ended and I looked at him and smiled.

He looked at me in a sort of disbelief. "Yo, it is so crazy that your mind goes there."

Dammit. "Well, I am a girl ya know, so I naturally notice those things. The only thing I could see was her nails and I really did almost get that color, so I was just glad that I didn't."

He wasn't mad at all. "I know girls notice shit like that, but you more than anybody I know. That's why I knew that if we were going to do this, I had to be able to be completely honest with you about everything, because you would find out anyway."

Sis, I have no idea what came over me in that moment. I don't know what type of angel or devil was on my shoulder whispering in my ear telling me what to say, but out of nowhere, I had a very important question. "Are you guys married?" I looked him right in his eyes when I asked.

He looked away but he answered at the same time. "Yes." He nodded his head yes too.

I felt like I got shot in the heart. Like right then, he punched me in my chest as hard as he could. Do you know how exhausting it is to constantly have to hold your shit together because the same nigga keeps shocking you with news that tops the last round? I placed my elbows on the table, put my head down and said, "Fuck." I didn't yell it or anything. It was literally like an exhale that came out in order to prevent myself from crying. Immediately after, I looked up at him. "I thought you wanted a big wedding? Did you have a wedding?" Those questions were completely irrelevant but they came out of my mouth so quickly. There was no going back, so I waited for an answer.

He didn't even make eye contact with me. I don't know where he was looking or what he was looking at, but it wasn't at me. "Nah, we just went to the courthouse."

I tucked my lips into my mouth and nodded in understanding. "That's deep." Those were the only words I could find and then I had to put my hands underneath my legs because I could see them shaking.

"I'm just a country nigga, you know?" He finally looked at me.

That was a confusing statement because he was as city as it gets. No connection with City Girls. "What does that even mean?" Before he even had a chance to respond, it dawned on me. "Oh, marry her because she's pregnant." My eyes were stuck. They weren't looking at him, they were just stuck in a daze while I aimlessly nodded my head back and forth. "Well, congrats. I guess."

Mark leaned back in his chair a little. "No, not congrats. I don't think you say congrats for something I was going to do. I told you before that I was probably going to marry her, I just didn't plan on doing it this soon. But you have to remember, part of our script on our show is that she was celibate until marriage and being that marriage licenses are public knowledge, we went to the courthouse and got it done. I wanted to make sure she was able to keep her reputation, so it wasn't a big thing."

I stood up after that. "Gotcha." That was the only word I could find. None of this made sense to me. I knew that Mark could tell I was trying to keep my shit together because he was trying to be abnormally funny. That wasn't like him, but the situation had completely changed my energy and I was trying hard not to emit the energy I really felt. I started to walk toward the counter to grab my purse and phone and then my keys from different places around my apartment and headed toward the front door. There's a little counter near the door, so I placed everything there and started to put my shoes on. He was still sitting down at the table trying to figure out what I was doing. I looked up at him and put on my best fake smile. "Wanna come get food with me?" I knew good and well that wasn't going to happen, but I also knew I needed to be away from him.

He got up from the table and checked his pockets to be sure he had everything. "Nah, shorty. Do your thing. I gotta get to the mall." He walked over to the door and began putting his shoes on.

We both finished at the same time but at that moment I didn't even want to walk out the door with him. "Aw man, I need to go potty." So I started to take my shoes off again. Once they were off, I turned to hug him before he left. Once I gave him the hug, he didn't let me go, but I had taken my arms from around his neck. When I tried to move, he just held my waist tighter, so I looked at him and rolled my eyes and threw my head back dramatically.

When I looked at him again, he kissed me. I didn't even close my eyes because I wasn't even prepared for that. We hadn't kissed in years! I just learned he was married and I had just watched a video of his wife showing him the 3D ultrasounds of their unborn child. After the first kiss, I just looked at him with a super confused face. Then, he lifted my chin and kissed me for real. Not just a peck, a real kiss with passion and tongue. I looked at him and shook my head and covered my face with my hand. "Why are you like this?" I was so confused but I also had a slight smile on my face.

He smiled at me. "Love you, shorty. Go get you some food." He was so casual when he said that and then he just walked out of the door.

I had no intentions of leaving my house to go get food. I literally just needed him out so that I could begin processing everything that had happened prior to the kiss and the I love you. Once the latter happened, I needed him out of my space completely because I needed all the oxygen in the room to myself.

When I closed the door, I locked it and then stood on my toes to look through the peephole. My intentions were to make sure he was absolutely out of sight before I fell apart. There were no tears this time; I don't think I had anymore tears left to cry. There was a pit in my stomach, so when he was out of my view through the peephole, I turned around, leaned my back against the door and slid my body down until I was sitting on the ground. I sat there, crisscross applesauce, hands in my lap, and just looking into space.

My thoughts were moving faster than they ever had before. Why did he kiss me? Why did he say he loves me? Why did he show me those ultrasounds? Why in the entire fuck did he not tell me they got married! I laughed a little to myself and shook my head in disbelief. It was New Year's Eve and this nigga just kissed me and then went to the mall to buy an outfit for the night he would spend with his wife. I said, "What is life?" out loud.

For what felt like the first time in my entire life, I was incapable of processing the information given to me. The only things I knew for sure were that Mark was in way over his head by trying to basically have a wife and a girl-friend because he was never the type of guy to be able to be emotionally involved with two separate women in the same capacity.

I also knew that he was playing a very sick mind game with me; it just didn't make sense why he was doing that because he had everything he wanted in Brittany Vasquez. She was his best friend, his lover, his business partner, his child's step mother and soon to be mother of his next child. He didn't need me, especially not how he was trying to deal with me. I also knew that for some unknown reason, he deliberately kept the fact that he was married away from me and that was the most insulting part of it all.

The more I thought about it, I started to remember that I would see a ring on his finger in pictures on social media. I jumped up from the floor and rushed to the counter where my phone was. Once the phone was unlocked, I went to his page and read through his comments and low and behold, whenever a fan would comment about how he should marry her, he would tell them he already did. Like, what the fuck! Anyway, I sat down and really leveled with myself and by the time I was done, I concluded that I wasn't even allowed to feel any type of way about anything that had just transpired.

The man that I was secretly in love with was cheating on what I now know to be his wife of less than six months. Why would I ever think that he would be honest with me about anything? I guess I sort of appreciated the fact that he was honest when I asked, but I also felt entitled to having that information voluntarily given to me, especially since it was clearly social media knowledge.

As I sit here and tell you this fucked up story, I wish I would have kept it all the way funky with myself: you are a sidebitch, you aren't entitled to entitlements. As crazy as this sounds, I had decided not to address any of it in that moment. I wanted to give myself a few days to see how I felt and then move forward from there.

I left this little gem out but, during that time of healing after the miscarriage, the pregnancy news, the whole fall out with Mark, in general, I met a music executive named Chris. I can't lie, he resembled Mark in appearance, but we all have a type. I actually met him at the gas station one morning and he very politely told me I was beautiful. You see, I have a thing for smooth niggas. Doesn't matter what you say to me, it's all about how you say it and he articulated it very eloquently, so I gave him my number when he asked for it. We talked on the phone regularly, both *FaceTime* and regular, and always had really good conversations.

Chris was very intriguing, therefore, he had no

problem keeping my attention but since I was in a stage of healing at the time we met, I made sure we took it really slow. Shockingly, I never had to tell him I wanted to move slow, he just knew and respected my unspoken wishes so there was never any pressure for me to spend time with him. The thing that attracted me to him was that he was like a classy-hood nigga. That basically means that he was intelligent, well-spoken, intellectual, all about his money but still had some hood nigga qualities to him. Not to mention he had big dick energy. We were taking it slow and hadn't actually seen each other since we met, so I didn't know what lil daddy was really working with. Anyway, in the midst of my common chaos in regard to Mark, Chris called me. Honestly, it was a breath of fresh air to see his name on my phone because his energy was always so peaceful and I needed that more than ever at that moment. When I finally answered the phone, I had a big smile on my face. "Hi," I said in my girlie, I'm about to cake with my boo, voice.

He was obviously in the car. "Hey, gorgeous. What you on?"

There was no way in hell I was about to tell him I just experienced yet another earth-shattering moment with my on again/off again boo that wasn't actually my boo because he has a pregnant wife but somehow loves me and doesn't want to lose me after I had already loved him for the last four years. So, instead, I said, "Nothing, about to go get some food. Wanna go eat with me?" Clearly, my life was a roller-coaster so I just needed to handle every loop, turn and drop as best as I could. Chris was excited to see me after all this time, so I quickly changed my outfit because I smelled like Mark.

About forty-five minutes later, Chris picked me up from my house and we went to *Bossa Nova.* Naturally, he very gently attempted to get me to go to a New Year's Eve event with him, but I declined. I enjoyed his company, but I could also feel the weight of the other stuff starting to press down. Knowing myself the way that I do, I knew that it meant it was time to process everything. On the ride home, he massaged my neck and scalp while he drove. It was probably one of the most comforting things I had felt in a long time and I told myself that I was going to heal as quickly as I could so that I could give Chris a real opportunity.

E ither I had the itis or my mind was so exhausted that I just fell asleep as soon as I got home that night. Whatever the case, the countdown didn't stand a chance. I woke up to a HNY text from both Mark and Chris. I didn't respond to either of them right away. Instead, I got out of bed and started a bath, poured some peppermint lavender bath soak in the water, started the H.E.R station on my phone, undressed and stepped into the bathtub. It was the start of 2019 and I didn't want to begin the year off with any feelings or thoughts of negativity or confusion, so the determination to figure everything out before that bath water got cold, was my ultimate goal.

. . .

My first thoughts were obviously in regard to my situation with Mark. As I rubbed my feet over my smooth legs, I replayed the moment of me asking him about being married. I couldn't make sense of why he would withhold that information from me. For two entire months, we had spoken every single day about everything from getting laser hair removal to how parenting differs in our generation. For a second, I even started to question myself. Like, did I say or do something that would make him feel like sharing that information with me wasn't safe? That thought quickly vanished because it was absolutely absurd. He should have told me, period.

The only logical reason I could come up with is that he thought he would lose me even more if he told me, being that he knew how I felt about dealing with a man in a relationship, yet alone a married man. Although that concept made the most sense, it was still a sorry excuse. One thing Mark and anyone else knows about me is that I would prefer a painful truth over a pretty lie any day. Regardless of how much the truth hurts me, I can come back from it and I can maintain whatever respect I had for the messenger. A lie, on the other hand, whether it be withheld information or a blatant lie, literally makes me question every single thing that comes out of your mouth.

From there, my thoughts traveled to him kissing me. That kiss carried so much passion and intimacy when he did it. I couldn't decide if the kiss was because he knew he had fucked up by not telling me about the marriage before that moment, or if he would have kissed me that day whether or not we had the marriage conversation. Something in that thought triggered my emotions because a single tear rolled down my cheek and I didn't even bother to wipe it away. In that moment, there was no more processing to do because the right thing to do, if not for myself but for his pregnant wife, was to sever all ties with him.

The friendship that we had built or strengthened over the last two months really meant a lot to me, however, the extracurricular activities, the emotions that were starting to come out of the box I packed them in, and the emotional change I was starting to see in Mark needed to come to an end. There was no way for me to figure out how long it would take or even where to start, but I decided that I needed to fall out of love with Mark so that I could try to be a platonic friend and not feel any sort of emotion when I see or hear about him and his wife.

The tricky part was that I wasn't sure if a platonic friendship was possible once I stopped being in love with him. On the other hand, I knew that the pain associated with falling out of love would end at some point. Whereas, the pain I would have felt if I stayed in that situation would have grown deeper. In some sick way, I could have possibly normalized the sidebitch role in my mind. Normalizing that situation would have been so detrimental to my sanity, so I knew ending it all was the best bet and it needed to be done by the end of January – no excuses.

· · ·

S ee, Chris was a really good guy. He was doing well for himself, had the character traits of a leader, he was patient with me and was fine. He wasn't going to wait much longer. Being that I spent time with him on New Year's Eve, I think I extended my stay, for at the very least, one more month. Breaking it off with Mark in that time, would perfect. By the time I came to all of my solutions or resolutions, my water was starting to get cold, so I drained the bathtub and started a hot shower. If you don't take a shower after you take a bath, what are you doing?

Once I got out of the shower, I texted Chris back first. 'Same to you, sir. Thank you for hanging out with me yesterday. Thank you for just being you, in general. I know I'm kinda sorta frustrating because I keep you at such a distance, but I just want you to know that I appreciate your patience. I came from a lot when I met you, so I didn't want to ruin you while I was ruined.

But I'm okay now, so I'm going to try my best to give you more of me.' I must have read that message seventeen times before I hit send because I was so nervous. Anxiety crept in because what if it was too dramatic? I finally hit send and locked my phone. From there, I dried my body off, put on some pajama shorts and a sports bra and headed to the restroom to do a face mask and lip scrub. That day was all about cleansing and clarity because I wanted my year to be clean and clear.

. . .

Before I began applying my face mask, I texted Mark back. His message was simple, 'Same to you, sir.' Then I put my phone face down on the counter. Instantly, I felt an odd sense of relief even though I hadn't officially ended things yet. It just felt good knowing that I had come to a conclusion and that each conflicting thought would dissolve over the next month. I guess I felt free even though I didn't ever feel trapped.

The rest of my day was relaxing, to say the least. My friends and I *FaceTimed* each other to wish one another a Happy New Year and I cooked a full Sunday dinner for myself. Whenever I cook, whoever wants to come over and eat is welcome. I sent out a group text to let everyone know that there was black eyed peas, rice, mac and cheese, collard greens and fried chicken available to them. Since champagne is always my drink of choice, I drank an entire bottle, ate good and watched crime shows and fell asleep on the couch until three in the morning.

When I woke up, there was a text from Mark that said 'wyd'. The text was sent at eleven fifty-seven and typically I wouldn't send a text to his phone, especially at three in the morning because he has a whole wife, but that night, I didn't care. 'Just woke up. It doesn't make much of a difference, but I love you, Mark. Unconditionally. I don't know why you waited until you were married with a baby on the way to love me back, but you did. I need to let you go. I need to fall out of love with you and love you with only philia love. I shouldn't feel entitled to information about your personal life and I should be happy for you and your blessings without any reservations.

I don't know how long it will take me to fall out of love with you but I have to start now and I hope that once it happens, I am able to be your friend. Honestly, I don't know if I will be able to do that but I have to at least try. Loving you this deeply hurts me and I don't want to feel this way. I don't deserve this. I don't deserve less than half of you and that's all you can give me. I deserve somebody that can fall in love with me like I am with him. You are not in love with me and you cannot be in love with me. There is no forever for us in what we're doing.' I read the text again to check for typos and then I hit send.

There was no way for me to know how he would respond to that because we were more in a relationship than we had ever been and I was basically breaking up with him. At the same time, what could he really say? He was married, with a child on the way. You can't fight for your girlfriend to stay when you have a wife at home. That being said, without expecting a response, I moved from the couch to my bed to continue my champagne sleep.

At four thirty-three in the morning, I woke up to the sound of my doorbell going crazy. Initially, I was scared because I wasn't expecting anybody to be at my house and no one would ring my doorbell that way at that hour. Truth be told, I was even scared to step foot out of my bed, but the sound was so irritating, I grabbed the hammer that was hidden underneath my bed and used just the background light of my phone to guide me to the door. I didn't want to turn any actual lights on because I didn't want the psycho at my door to see that anyone was home. Hesitantly, I stepped to the door and looked through the peephole to see Mark standing at my door. My first thought was thank God. Then I thought, what the hell? While I took a deep breath, I put the hammer down in the corner because I didn't even know what I was about to do with it and then I opened the door.

A s soon as I opened the door, I looked up at him and he instantly grabbed me by my face and throat and guided me backwards to the wall inside the door while the door closed behind him. He wasn't gripping my face hard, but I placed my hand on his wrist and kept my eyes on his until the door closed and removed any light that was shining through. Once the door closed, he lifted my head lightly and began kissing me really hard. Naturally, I was kissing him back before I realized what was happening and then I pulled my head back and put my chin down.

There's a light switch right next to the front door, so I flipped it on and looked at him and pushed him back a little. This entire scene was right out of movie and was brand new territory for Mark. I wasn't even sure what question to ask first; all I could do was look at him with my hands out and my eyebrows shifted. Finally, I found my words. "Mark Garnett! What are you doing?" I walked away from him and toward my bedroom and he quickly followed. I don't know why this mattered, but as he followed me, I stopped in my tracks and turned around and said, "Take your shoes off!" I was mad at him but at that very moment, I wasn't exactly sure why I was mad.

We finally made it to my room. When he got in the room, he was taking his phone and wallet out of his pockets and putting them on the side table as if he was staying for a while. Emotional exhaustion took over my body. I transitioned from anger to hurt in what felt like seconds. Fucking emotional roller-coaster. I crossed my arms in front of my body and sat at the edge of my bed. "Mark." I rolled my eyes and shook my head in disappointment. "What are you doing here?"

He started to take his hoodie off, so his face was covered while he responded. "You're not leaving me. You're mine. I love you. I'm in love with you. I didn't wait until I was married to feel that way, or whatever the fuck your message said. Whatever it said, stop saying that shit. You're not leaving. I don't care what other nigga can be in love with you because I'm in love with you! You think you fucking know everything and you don't! You're wrong about how I feel about you at least half the time.

Why do you want to fight this so bad? Why can't you just accept the fact that we're in some shit? You have nothing to lose here. Nothing. I am literally risking it all for you because if Brittany found out about this it, will fuck everything up. You think I'm risking everything for somebody I'm not in love with? Just fucking trust me! Some shit is better left unsaid, but you just have to know everything all the time. You're not leaving me, Kiana."

. . .

His demeanor started to change from super turned up to defeated, but I hadn't even said a word. I wasn't even looking at him.

"I need you, Ki. I need you now and I need you forever. you can't leave." He stepped closer to me and lifted my chin so that I was looking up at him, but I kept my eyes down. "Look at me." He said softly.

"Please."

In the entire four years that I had known this man, I had never shed a single tear in front of him. Every tear that I ever cried was in private or over the phone where he couldn't see me. That night, there was no holding it together. There was no being strong. There was no hiding emotions. Tears raced down my face uncontrollably and I gently moved his hand from my chin and covered my face with my own hands. He just stood there in front of me waiting for who knows what.

Originally, I was sitting at the edge of my bed, so I moved further back, crossed my legs and with a face wet with tears, I looked at him. "Why are you doing this to me? You're not in love with me. You lust me. You like the fact that you can fuck me and get your dick sucked and I won't tell your wife. You're selfish! You have everything you want at home with your perfect partner and your perfect relationship, so why won't you just let me let you go? You can fuck any bitch you want and I'm sure you can even find one that won't tell your wife too. What am I getting out of this besides hurt? You think good dick and an hour of your time every day is enough? I can't depend on you for shit, you know why? Because you're married!!! There's a whole piece of you unavailable to me and my needs, wants and desires because it belongs to your wife." My tears had dried up by that point because I was starting to get mad again. "Your fucking pregnant wife!! You waited 'til you got her pregnant and married her to love me! For what? We can never even do simple shit together again. We can't go to breakfast, we can't go to Target, I can't even so much as wear my man's hoodie around because you're not my man! You're Brittany's man!"

S adness filled my heart and I began to cry again. "You are giving me less than half of you, Mark. Less than half! As your friend, do you not think I deserve more than that? Or are you so selfish that as my lover, you don't give a fuck? It's not fair." I started shaking my head in disbelief. "It's not–"

He climbed onto the bed and bear-hugged me and my silent tears turned into uncontrollable weeping which prevented me from finishing whatever I had left of my impromptu speech. In that moment, I wasn't even thinking of anything, I could only feel, and all I felt was hurt.

Mark was basically coddling me at that point. He was hugging me and wiping my tears away at the same time. "I hate seeing you like this. I hate that I'm the reason you're like this right now. I'm sorry. You're right. I'm selfish but I can't help it, Ki. I love you more than you know. I need you more than you know. Life doesn't always make sense to me but we make sense to me. I wanna make it make sense for you but I don't know how because I can't tell you everything. I just need you to trust me. I can make it mutually beneficial. I'll start paying every single one of your bills, I'll put up whatever money you need to start your company exactly the way you want to – just stay, please."

We were face to face at that point, not hugging anymore, but I wasn't looking at him, I was looking down at my hands.

"Ki, look at me. Tell me you'll stay."

My eyes were closed tight as I tried to prevent more tears from streaming down my face. My head was still shaking in disbelief. "You don't get it. I don't care about the money, Mark! I care about you! I want you! All of you, not just a piece of you and I can never have that. You married someone else." I started to laugh through my tears.

"Even if your marriage didn't work, you chose her, not me. I'm not a sidebitch, Mark. I am a wife and I have no clue how you can't see that but it doesn't matter, because you have already chosen your wife. I can't stay. What type of woman am I for dealing with not just a married man but a married man whose wife is pregnant. That's shitty. I'm not shit for that and karma is going to come so hard. What happens if you get caught? Then what? She isn't going to leave you. So, where does that leave me? Alone? While you get to keep your family and drop me because that's where your priority and loyalty lie. That means I'm disposable, here. Meanwhile, there's men out there willing to make me their wife and I'm stuck on another woman's husband."

R ight then and there, I became too tired mentally, emotionally and physically to continue. "Mark, stop. We have to stop. This is insane. I need to go to bed. Please. We have to stop."

I started to make my way off the bed and grabbed his stuff so that he could put it back in his pockets. He started to get off the bed too. He grabbed his phone from me and started to text. I didn't know who or what he was texting, but then my phone alerted me of a text message. It was a *CashApp* notification.

Five thousand dollars. Mr. Miller, as the text said, sent you five thousand dollars. I threw my phone back on the bed.

"Mark!" I gave him a death stare. My momma didn't raise no fool, so I wasn't going to send it back.

He grabbed his hoodie off the floor and put it back on. "Even if you say no, keep that. Please." He kissed my forehead. "Please don't leave me, Kiana." He paused and looked at me and shook his head like he had some sort of clarity from all of this. "I need you." He walked out of the room and I didn't even follow because I knew he would lock the door on his way out. I turned the light off, climbed back into my bed underneath the blankets, and curled up into the fetal position. I didn't think about anything, I didn't attempt to process anything, I just cried myself to sleep.

The next morning, I didn't wake up until about eleven and I was in the same position I was when I had fallen asleep that night. I could feel my puffy eyes and my head was pounding. The headache could have been from the bottle of champagne or the crying, probably a nice little cocktail of both. I grabbed my phone off the side table because the first thing I thought about was Mark sending me a five-thousand-dollar *CashApp* in the middle of our storm. The cash was definitely in my *CashApp* and I can't lie to you, it felt pretty fucking incredible. You know me, logic started to kick in, so I had to catch my thoughts as quickly as I could. Want to know a few of the thoughts I caught? Okay, *Would any sane man pay a woman five thousand dollars a month just so that he could have sex with her? Like, is Brittany boring in bed or what? Well, she is carrying a whole human, so it can't be that boring.*

Niggas can pull out of boring pussy. Mark might actually be in love with me. He has never just pulled up unannounced and he has never fought for me to stay. Damn, what if my theory is right? What if he really just married her because it made the most sense financially and now he stays for the same reason? Is staying and sending me five thousand dollars a month cheaper than leaving? This nigga thinks I can be bought, fuck him! However, it's kinda lit that all of my money would be mine, because he would be paying all of my bills. Who knows how long this will last, but it's one hell of an offer because my business launch would be super lit too. However many months it lasts, I could just make sure I save at least half of what he gives me and half of what I make on my own. I can't even believe I'm considering taking this deal. Money really is the root to all evil.

T hose were really just my warm up thoughts, you're going to die when you hear what I finally decided to do. Before I got out of bed that morning, I decided that I was going to trade in love for business. The fact of the matter was that having Mark in my life hurt me just as much as not having him in my life at all. All of the things that hurt me and all of the things that I enjoyed were all being experienced for free. I kept letting him back in for free. I kept entertaining his bullshit and ignoring his lies for free.

So, I decided to take his offer. I knew I was going to have to figure out the quickest way to pull my feelings out of the game because I wasn't giving anything away for free anymore. Even though I knew sidebitch wasn't my role, I was about to level up off that role. I told myself that I would wait until he contacted me again to determine whether or not he was really serious and I would lay out a few ground rules in an attempt to protect myself moving forward. It was already noon by that time, so I got out of bed to shower and get my life together.

He texted me at about two-thirty that afternoon.

'Hey you.' No one tests the water before they dive in more than Mark does. I was annoyed by that because I just wanted him to say whatever it is he had to say.

Irritated, I kept my response short. 'Hey.'

He knew I was bothered, but proceeded anyway. 'You ok?'

The conversation was moving too slow for me, so I decided to just give him exactly what he was looking for. 'That's a silly question. I don't even know who you were last night and I think you're nuts. Absolutely insane. You're married. Why are you fighting so hard for me to stay? Why are you willing to pay? What are you not telling me? None of this makes sense to me. I don't understand why I am so crazy in love with you or why I can't let you go, so for now, I will stay. The money isn't going to make any of it easier for me emotionally, but it's incentive and that's annoying. I am still going to date other people, but I won't have sex with them unless I decide that the contract they are offering can buy me out of this contract. By that, I mean someone offering me real love and everything I deserve from a man. I don't want to be blindsided by any other milestones in your life. That means, if your wife knows, I need to know too. If the media knows, I need to know before that. I can't even believe I'm typing any of this.'

Believe it or not, I sent that message.

It took him no time to respond. His response was straight to the point, all he sent was a big smiley face emoji.

I can't imagine what it must have been like for him to

have that huge blow up with me and then go home and act like his life was perfectly fine when he got in bed next to his wife. Back then, I learned very quickly not to carry the weight of anything that was not mine to carry. How he dealt with things when he got home was always going to be his issue and never mine.

The next eleven months of my life were a whirlwind. On the second of every single the month, without me ever having to ask, Mark sent me five thousand dollars. Now, you and I are basically best friends at this point, so I have to keep it all the way real with you, I didn't save a dime during those first three months. First, I put ten thousand dollars on a year old white *BMW X6* with tinted windows and black rims. I mean, I deserved it. My interactive website, logo and merchandise for my creative agency were all done perfectly. My launch party was super lit.

After the launch party, my clientele list skyrocketed and I was doing at least three events a month, which then started to make it really easy for me to start saving. Obviously, I needed a house next. You would think that since I seemingly had the world at my fingertips, I would have had a crazy roster of men, but I didn't. Chris and I continued to grow closer and spend more time together. Unfortunately, I don't do the multiple sex partner thing, so I lied to Chris and told him I was celibate. It was hard because some days I would look at myself in the mirror and think that I was no better than Mark was for cheating on his wife.

They had the baby, obviously, and Mark was ecstatic. The day Brittany gave birth, he sent me a text that simply said, 'she's here.' That was pretty hard for me, but what was I going to do? I had literally signed up for that. I asked for a picture of the baby and told him congratulations. Before the baby arrived, Mark had made a very conscious effort to come see me at least three times a week. We also spoke on the phone at least three times a day and we DM'd regularly throughout the day. As much as I hate to say this, we had a system that was working out well for us.

He scaled back on telling me things I didn't need to know about his little marriage, but he made sure to tell me everything I needed to know or had the ability to find out. That made it easier for me to handle certain situations, not that anything huge happened other than the baby. He knew about Chris because I wanted to give him the same respect I expected him to give me when it came to honesty and transparency. Beyond that, if Chris and I were going to get serious-serious, I didn't want Mark to feel blindsided when I ended our contract. Of course, he didn't like the idea of any of it, but, as I always mentioned, he was married with a new baby.

My friends all thought it was insane that I had this double life thing going on, but they also were like, "Get your bag, sis." Even crazier than that, even my mom understood. Mark was really in love with me and it hurt me to my core because I still loved him too, but I knew that I would have to bring it all to an end eventually.

Eight months in and I started having sex with Chris. My feelings for him were nowhere near as deep as they were with Mark, but I started to feel like if I didn't have Mark, I could start to feel that deeply for Chris. The other thing is that I was basically lying to Chris because he never knew about Mark and on top of that, I never told Mark that I started having sex with Chris. It was all becoming such an exhausting experience. Truthfully, I don't know how Mark did it.

In December, I finally sat down with Mark and told him that I wanted to give my situation with Chris a real chance. It was obvious that I still loved him but I couldn't be a mistress forever; it was nowhere near realistic for me. Understandably, Mark was hurt and upset, but he handled it a lot better than I thought he would and asked me if we could still talk once or twice a week. I agreed to that because I figured that it would eventually fade itself out.

TWELVE

SELF REFLECTION

ONE OF MY greatest internal battles is vulnerability. I have an immense fear of being vulnerable to or with the wrong person. The fear lies in giving someone a piece of me that they can later use against me. Even deeper than that sometimes, I even fear being vulnerable with myself. Sometimes, allowing myself to feel through the deepest part of my pain, is too painful. I've conditioned myself to be strong. Stand tall. Head always high. Never let them see you cry. I've never thought tears to equate to lack of strength; not in men or women. But I will say that my desire to always be strong has become poison to my spirit. It poisoned me because somehow the idea of being vulnerable has become more frightening than powerful to me, but only for myself. I say only for myself because I am a safe haven for others' vulnerability. I pride myself on the fact that people are openly vulnerable with me. It makes me feel like they feel safe here. So, the fact that I fear so greatly doing the same, blows me.

Throughout this time, allowing myself to play the role of a sidebitch was draining. I was emotionally and mentally exhausted. I would find myself sitting in traffic with tears streaming down my face and I literally couldn't even pinpoint one exact reason why I was crying. Some nights, I would wake up in the middle of the night with wet hair and a wet pillow because I had been crying in my sleep. How did I get here? How could I love myself so much, think so highly of me and work so hard to become this woman and still only amount to a sidebitch. Even deeper than that, how did I allow myself to be demoted to a sidebitch. I was disgusted with myself.

The conflicting thoughts of him actually loving me but choosing his career versus just being played because I was a safe space to get his dick wet, were thoughts that I couldn't shake. It made me feel insane because how could I feel two totally different feelings behind the same action. I felt dumb. I felt powerless. I felt small. I felt these things in some part because him never choosing me made me feel that way, and in some part was due to my own insecurities that I wasn't even aware existed until I started participating in this role. Maybe they didn't exist before this? Maybe they were created because of this?

Like I had told Mark, I never once felt like I had one up on Brittany. I never felt like I had any part of him other than the ability to make his dick hard without even touching him. I never felt any sense of entitlement to his time, energy, spirit or mind. I never felt superior to her in any way. Not that I should have. I've just seen women in the past boast about having someone else's man. I never felt that way. Maybe I never felt that way because I don't embody that type of malice in my heart? Maybe I didn't feel that way because I feel like at one point, he was my man or maybe I didn't feel that way because part of me feels like he was never my man?

I still haven't been able to figure that part out; I probably never will. Of course, none of that justifies my actions. Even then, it didn't make me feel better about what I was doing. In fact, I genuinely believe knowingly being a sidebitch is by far worse than involuntarily being one due to your lack of knowledge of the actual girlfriend or wife. Crazy because when he and I first started, I blatantly said I would never willingly share my man. Ironically, there I was knowingly sharing someone else's man.

There were a number of times where I felt like he was in over his head. I felt like he didn't truly understand the depth of the game he was playing because I think it felt so easy for him at first. Think about it, he had two beautiful, powerful, God-fearing women in his corner. One he lived with and created an entire family with, while the other quietly sat on the sidelines eager to play whenever she was given the chance. I made it easy for him. I am the reason he cheated on his girlfriend for months and the reason that five months into his marriage, he cheated on his wife. The fact of the matter is that men wouldn't cheat as often if women wouldn't let them.

The truth is, I loved him. Deeply and unconditionally. Saying that out loud makes me feel like a clown; the entire fucking circus. How could I love a man who never chose me? How could I love a man that did not belong to me? If I'm honest with you, I think that we were soulmates. The problem was that he had chosen his life partner. It's okay that he did. I mean, it has to be, there is no other option. Besides, I wanted him to be truly happy. Even if that meant I wasn't a part of that happiness. Beyond that, even if they didn't work out, I'm pretty sure I wouldn't have been able to be in a real relationship with him. I think I draw the line at having a baby on me.

But who knows, I also thought I drew the line at a man that has a girlfriend...and here we are. He basically just erased every line I've ever drawn. I told you, I don't think that he was in love with her, but I do believe that he loved her. I think that had it not been for her father being able to put him back in a position to do exactly what he loves, and her creativity creating content for the *Zeus Network*, thus putting money in his pocket, their story would have ended at 'friends'.

Sometimes we allow what someone has done for us, be an anchor to our entire life. We let our loyalty to the feeling of being grateful hold us hostage instead of being grateful, paying dues, staying in contact but continuing to live our lives our way. That's what I think Mark did. I think that he got so caught up in being grateful for the opportunity his relationship with Brittany afforded him, and the platform the *InstaSeries* had given him, that he just ignored reality. I mean, he doesn't even play basketball anymore. He's basically a full-time actor and professional Mr. Vasquez.

Even though it hurt me for a while today, I'm okay with that. I believed in Mark's talent, sometimes more than he believed in it himself. I wish that he hadn't allowed his relationship to overshadow his career, but I am glad that he was able to rebuild his life from what it was when I met him. No matter what, I have only ever wanted to see him win.

At this point, I'm sure you think I'm an entire fool. You probably think I am weak and that if I did it once, I'd do it again. You are certainly entitled to your opinion because I have shared a piece of my life with you. My truth is mine and I will always live in it, whether I am right or wrong — it's about accountability. I know that I should have stopped dealing with Mark as soon as I knew he and Brittany were a couple. Hell, I probably should have stopped dealing with him years before that, when he said he couldn't be in a relationship. But I didn't.

Moving past having dealt with him while he had a girlfriend, I took a deal and dealt with him after he married her. In hindsight, I can be bought. I accepted five thousand dollars a month for an entire year to do something I knew was wrong. There's two things about that. One, I didn't care that it was wrong by society's standards, only that it was wrong by my standards. Two, I had done it for free for so long, I might as well have accepted payment to put myself in a better position. Does it make it better? Maybe not. Does it make it right? Absolutely not.

I grew a lot during that time. I think that some of my greatest strength came from the entire four years I spent in and out of turmoil with Mark. He is still an incredible father, but instead of being a father to two girls and a boy, he is doing an incredible job at balancing two careers and co-parenting with two women in order to raise and teach two little princesses how to be queens. His marriage didn't work out but it appears that he and Brittany are co-parenting cordially. I see him from time to time at public events and sometimes at little things our mutual friends have for the group, like game night, etc. Whenever we see each other, we have casual small talk. There is no bad blood between us.

Once, at a game night Stephon had, he pulled me aside to tell me that he was sorry for ever hurting me. He told me that he wished things could have ended differently between us. There wasn't really much for me to say other than thank you. There isn't really much to that, it happened the way it did and we are where we are now. Whenever he and I run into each other, wherever we are, I make sure to tell my boyfriend about the encounter. Although Mark and I have so much history, I never want to give him the ability to have any information about me that my man doesn't already have. I mean, the same way no man of mine should ever allow the streets to tell me anything about him that he hasn't already told me, I will never allow the streets to tell my man anything before me.

As for me, I'm happy. Chris and I are in a great space and we continue to grow and operate as a unit, which is refreshing. He's transparent with me about everything I need to know and vice versa. This is the first time I've ever experienced a healthy love. One where we communicate properly and I'm being loved exactly the way I want and deserve to be. It's so fulfilling to wake up each day and find new ways to love the man that loves me. Knowing that I am his and he is mine. I know how karma works, though, so I just hope that he respects me enough not to fall in love with the bitch he cuts a deal with.

CONNECTING

Let's connect. You can find me on social media at the handles listed. Don't be afraid to alert me of your presence by sending a message.

www.lowkee.info

facebook.com/lowkeeauthor

twitter.com/   lowkee

instagram.com/___lowkee